High Praise for "The Sixty-first Minute!"

"Jesus Taught us by using parables. We may share the love of Christ in the same way. By putting Bill Thomas' book, *The 61st Minute* into the right hands, you may put that person on the path that will introduce him to the One he or she really needs to know."

—Chet Hanson
Author of *The Buyer*

"In *The 61st Minute*, Bill Thomas crafts a fascinating fictional account of last-minute reprieves and second chances, using the life and death of murderer Greg McBride. The theme, "It is never too late to come to Jesus," could be dull and preachy; instead, here it is tightly written and cleverly twisted back on itself to the very end."

—Mary Mueller
Author of *Stargazer*

"Ben Franklin tells us that time is the stuff life is made of, but Greg McBride is about to face the final minute of his life - an extra minute - a gift from God that will determine the fate of his eternity. *The 61st Minute* is worth the read, and will incite you to question and ponder the importance of every single minute of your life."

—Skip Coryell
Author of *Church and State*

Cover design created by Ron Bell of AdVision Design Group (www.advisiondesigngroup.com)

ISBN 978-1-61808-115-5
Library of Congress Control Number: 2015900658

Printed in the United States of America

White Feather Press

Making the world a better place – one reader at a time.

Dedication

To my friends at Northridge Church of Christ: may you continue to shine the light of Jesus Christ to those in darkness.

To the young men I worked with at Circleville Juvenile Correctional Facility: may you always remember that Jesus Christ offers a fresh start.

The Sixty-first Minute

Bill

Thomas

A Story of a Murderer Redeemed

Acknowledgements

I want to thank Skip and Sara Coryell for allowing my stories the chance to be seen and read. It is an honor to be a part of the family at White Feather Press and to promote Godly values and principles.

I am indebted to my editor, Nichole Ridner, who read this story more than anyone ever will, and sought to make it, not just a good book, but a vehicle to share the love and power of Jesus Christ. I pray that our efforts in this mission will touch lives. Thank you for your hard work, your dedication, your passion and your friendship.

I am grateful for Kari Hoyes, who reads what I write and checks the grammar to make it presentable. You've done that for me since I started writing and nobody does it better. Thank you.

I want to thank some good friends, Bob and Betty Jenkins and Becky Baxa, who were the first readers of this story and provided encouragement and insight as it was being written. Thanks also to Chris Strickland and Jim Landis, two of my co-workers, who also read this story early and helped promote the message.

Finally, I want to thank you, the reader. May you be blessed and encouraged. To God be the glory.

Prologue

It's been said that after the flood of Noah's time, the average life span of a man was shortened to about seventy years. Gregory Victor McBride did not reach that average. His death certificate indicates he died on June 12, 2013. He was fifty-six and a half years old when he was stabbed and bled to death in the Southeast Ohio Correctional Facility in Lucasville. His death was noted in the newspapers by a blurb in the regional news section. A few family members arranged for his body to be shipped to and buried in his hometown. For most people, that would be the final chapter of a story of a wasted life and missed opportunities.

But I know there's more to it.

Gregory Victor McBride lived fifty-six and a half years. That's just a bit over four hundred and ninety five thousand hours or nearly thirty million minutes. Does it seem strange that I've calculated his life to the hour or to the minute? I admit I find it odd, but fitting in this case. What is even more inexplicable is the one minute that is not listed among the thirty million. You read that correctly. Gregory Victor McBride got one extra minute, a sixty-first minute in the last hour of his life, that is not accounted for on his death certificate. In this "extra minute" is his remarkable story. I won't tell you it's true or it isn't. I'll simply tell his story as I promised I would. You decide what to make of it.

The 61st Minute

Chapter One

My name is Greg McBride, but for the last thirty years I've been known by the state of Ohio as #311572. That was my prison number. I'd been serving a life sentence in the Southeast Correctional Facility in Lucasville. I was one of over a thousand inmates who were listed as security level four. That's maximum security, but not the highest; that would be level five. To get here, I killed a man. I didn't think he was a particularly good man, but the state of Ohio didn't care about that. I was arrested, tried and found guilty. I arrived here after a short stint in a holding facility in the central part of the state. The day I came to Lucasville was a hot, July day thirty summers ago. Days drag by in a place like Lucasville. One day begins to look like the next. The seasons come and the seasons go. The calendar changes but not much else. Volunteers come in with various programs and then they leave. We never do. The monotony doesn't either. One day after another. They begin to look the same.

Right now, in the short time I have left, I need to tell you about my last day. It was a rainy, gray Wednesday morning. I'd been up for a couple of hours in my cell before the sunrise. My cell had a window, but you couldn't see through it; because it was too high on the wall and the bars blocked the view, but I could hear what was going on outside. The rain was coming down pretty hard. It was one of those early morning thunderstorms that ripped along the Ohio River dumping buckets in a matter of minutes. The heavy downpour and the sloppy mess that usually followed would probably prevent us from going into the yard. Fortunately, it was a Wednesday and that meant the chaplain would be offering a mid-week chapel service to anyone who wanted to attend and had not lost that privilege. I hadn't been a "religious" person for a long time. I went to chapel for one reason; business. You see, even behind the wire, a business could be built. Guys there wanted stuff. There's a word for it, contraband. Drugs, legal and illegal, along with a ton of other things, were always available, at the right price. I was a "businessman" on the outside and continued to work it on the inside as well. There's no need to go into how I was able to get supplies or inventory as I called it. You can do an internet search on how those things get into a prison facility. What mattered was I had the stuff other guys wanted and I intended to keep making money or bartering for better contraband.

I had some problems to take care of that Wednesday morning. Dempsey had reneged on his final payment for the pot I'd sent him through the pigeon, the messenger or courier of the prison who, for a small price, made discreet deliveries. Dempsey had to pay or my whole enterprise would be jeopardized. Two cells down from me was my "muscle guy," Big Tony. I supplied him a stash every two weeks and he made sure the rest paid. It was that simple. The rain would keep us from quietly taking care of things in the yard, so I decided to go to chapel. I sent the pigeon to tell Dempsey we'd meet him there. When the chaplain finished the last prayer, we expected him to drop off the cash. No excuses.

We trudged across the muddy yard around ten o'clock. Officer Hughes led a group of about six of us. Big Tony and I hung at the back of the group, as far as Hughes would let us. The sky was still gray, though it was mid-morning. I looked up at Big Tony. He looked straight ahead as we walked, determined as he always was. I also knew he was carrying a shank he'd made from the plastic casing of a ballpoint pen. He told me last night in the cafeteria that he was making a new one. I breathed a bit easier as we walked. I was carrying a considerable stash of money and some contraband, but if Big Tony was armed, I knew I was all right.

When we got to the chapel, there were already a dozen or so other inmates there. The chaplain was in the front of the makeshift sanctuary arranging a communion set. I saw Dempsey sitting with some of the others from his cellblock. We made eye contact, but only for a second or two. He knew I was there. The chaplain preached that day a message about the thief on the cross at the same time Jesus was crucified; not the first one that mocked Jesus, but the other one. He talked about getting a "second chance" and that this criminal, in his dying moment, turned to Jesus. It wasn't a bad message, I guess, but I was ready for it to be over. As soon as the final "Amen" had been said, I eased up to Dempsey. I knew Big Tony was right behind me. The guards were herding the inmates out of the chapel. There were a lot of people just milling around. There weren't as many security cameras in the chapel as there were in other places, so this made it a logical place to conduct business. The chaplain was still in the front, putting stuff away. Four or five guards were urging guys out. It had started raining again and this provided a brief moment of distraction. I had just a few seconds of unsupervised time, so I moved quickly to Dempsey.

"Hey," I said to him as I put my shoulder into his, "Where's the rest of what you owe me?"

Dempsey turned to face me and I looked into his bloodshot dark eyes.

"I don't owe you anything, you..."

Before he could finish, I turned my head to see if Big Tony had sprung into action.

He had the shank pulled from the cuff of his pants and was moving quickly. It happened so fast that I hardly knew what had gone down. I felt it though. He thrust the shank into my neck. I could feel blood, my blood, gushing down my chest. My orange prison issue was now crimson. I fell to the floor. I'd been double-crossed! A crowd of inmates gathered around as the noise of the commotion reached the rest of the room. Big Tony and Dempsey quickly took the money and contraband from me before the guards could push by the many prisoners who'd watched another violent attack without doing anything. I suppose there was chaos and confusion as the guards quickly moved to get the other inmates out of there and tried to establish who'd committed the violence. I can't be sure because, by this time, I was lying on the floor in a pool of blood. The whole incident happened in less than ten seconds. I could see the others being pushed out of the chapel. I knew security personnel were coming in as I could hear muffled voices. In those few moments of treachery and betrayal, I knew that my time was up. I was bleeding out and there was nothing anyone was going to be able to do. Though the flurry of activity blurred around me, one thing was clearly imprinted on my mind. *I'm going to die.* That thought terrified me. I'd killed a man, but here I was, afraid of dying myself. I knew that I wasn't ready for this. I'd heard from the time I was a boy about hell and dying apart from Jesus Christ. At one point, I'd made the good confession and been baptized. I meant it, too, at that time. But that was a long time ago. I'd strayed far from that little church in northern Ohio. I'd boasted throughout my adult life that I was looking forward to hell and partying with my friends and the devil. Now that outcome seemed likely and I wanted no part of it. I knew I only had minutes left in this world. Only minutes to try to turn things around. Though emergency personnel were kneeling beside me, trying to stop the bleeding, I hardly noticed them. A song kept coming to my mind; a child's song. *Jesus loves me. This I know. For the Bible tells me so.* Was it still possible? Could he still love me? I'd just heard about another criminal who had turned to Jesus in his dying moment. I knew my time was drawing to a close. A minute or two might be all I had left on this earth. I heard the paramedics say the pulse was feeble.

I couldn't speak audibly, but in my heart and mind my voice rang out. *Lord Jesus, please. Forgive me. Jesus.* I'm guessing that there were just seconds left of my life on earth as I made my final plea to heaven.

What happened next is incredible. I regained a sense of consciousness. I raised my head up without pain. I saw the medics next to me, but they weren't moving. I saw a few of the guards and prison administrators standing in the back of the room. The chaplain was leading a small group in prayer. It was like they were statues. Time seemed to stop. Everything and everyone was still. I looked around in disbelief. Was I dead? I heard a noise coming from the back of the room and that's when I saw her. A little girl no more than twelve was coming toward me. She wore a simple pink and white dress and brown sandals. She had short dark hair and a caramel complexion. She was obviously of Asian descent, most likely Korean I guessed.

She seemed to be unfazed by the statues around her. She moved through them without fear and came up to me.

"Hello. Are you Mr. Greg McBride?"

I stammered a bit. It all seemed so surreal.

"Yeah, kid. I am," I replied as I reached to touch my neck and noticed the bleeding had stopped.

"Good," she answered. "I've come for you."

I wasn't sure I'd heard her correctly.

"What was that again?" I asked as I stood.

She took my hand, looked up at me and smiled. She was a little vision of joy in a dark, gruesome place.

"You heard me. I'm here to get you; to take you."

She started walking, pulling me along, but I stopped.

"Hold on," I demanded as I dropped her hand.

"Take me where?"

"You cried out, didn't you," she asked. "I've been sent to help you. Come on. There isn't much time."

I looked around the room in which everything seemed to have stopped. It seemed strange, yet something about this little girl showing up seemed right.

"Okay," I said, taking her hand and heading to the door. "I'll go."

She smiled again.

"Hey," I asked her as we left the makeshift sanctuary, "what's your name?"

"Sun-Hi," she replied.

I'd heard what she said, but I stammered trying to say it.

"Sun, uh…"

"Sun-Hi," she corrected. "Try saying *Sunny,* like a 'sunny' day."

"Sun-Hi," I said as I smiled at her, "it's a pretty name."

"Thank you," she answered as we stepped out into the bright sunshine. "Let's hurry."

Sun-Hi led me out into the sunlit prison yard.

"What in the world happened?" I muttered. "It was raining something awful just a second ago."

"Things are different now, Mr. McBride," she answered. "We aren't exactly in the world you knew."

I walked with Sun-Hi through the grassy yard. The blood stains on my orange suit were gone.

We didn't see a soul. The cellblocks were all there as was the administration building. There just weren't any people around. We walked right through the door of the administration building and to the entry point of the facility. I was stunned when tiny Sun-Hi easily pulled open the heavy door that could only be unlocked electronically by a guard behind a glass wall. I walked in silence next to this strange little girl as we stepped out of the prison entrance and into the free world. She continued to hold my hand as she led me to the parking lot and if she hadn't, I might've made a run for it. The free world! It had been so long. Sun-Hi released my hand as we approached an old Jeep Wrangler.

"Get in, Mr. McBride," she said as she jumped in. "You drive. I will tell you where we need to go."

I climbed in the driver's side of the jeep, found the key in the ignition and started the engine.

"Okay now, little lady," I said as I started to ease the jeep through the abandoned parking lot, "just where are we supposed to go?"

She fastened her seatbelt and looked up at me; her intense brown eyes seemed to look deeply into my soul.

"Mr. McBride," she started.

"Please," I interrupted, "Just call me Greg."

"Okay, Greg," she continued, "I've been sent as an answer to your prayer. You cried out to the Lord in your final seconds of life on this earth. He heard you and he has an answer for you. He loves you and wants you to be with him. However, he has something to show you first. There are some things you need to know, people you need to meet and an important task you need to do. So, Greg, you've been given a rare gift. You get an extra minute to change the world."

Her words left me dazed. The jeep just idled at the entrance to the parking lot of the prison I'd known as "home" for thirty years. *Did the Lord really hear me? How could this girl be an answer for anything? What did she mean by an extra minute? What could I do for the Lord or anybody else for that matter?*

Sun-Hi nudged my arm.

"Come on, Greg. Let's go. There isn't a lot of time."

"Where should we go, Sun-Hi?" I asked, not really sure if I wanted to know how she would answer.

"Euclid," she told me.

"Euclid," I stammered. "That's where I grew up."

"Yes," she replied. "That's our first stop."

Chapter Two

The drive from Lucasville to Euclid should've taken almost five hours, but time seemed to stop. I wasn't sure if time even mattered in the world I found myself in. Normally there would be traffic piled up on I-71, but as we drove it this time, it was deserted. That was unusual, but then again, so was this whole thing. All kinds of signs dotted the highway noting cities or towns. I'd never heard of some of the restaurants and gas stations advertised on many of them. Sun-Hi didn't say much throughout the drive, so I was left alone with only my thoughts to sort through. *What just happened? Was I already dead and this a cruel joke? Maybe the whole thing is a dream; a nightmare. Who is this girl in this strange situation with me? She keeps talking about God and Jesus, but I haven't thought about them in years. Why would I go back to Euclid? There's nothing there for me. This whole thing is crazy!* Many times I was tempted to take an exit off the highway, push this little girl out of my life and see what was going on. As I contemplated that plan, I'd look over at Sun-Hi and she'd smile. Something about her smile, innocence and insistence put those thoughts to rest. I continued north to my hometown.

Euclid was a suburb of Cleveland. At one time it had been a very nice community, and I'm sure there are still some parts of it that are nice, but the neighborhood I grew up in was tough. Drugs, gangs, violence and death were common. For a young man to live into his twenties was a fifty/fifty proposition at best. I was about three when we moved there, just after my sister, Amber was born. My father worked at the post office and my mother stayed at home with my sister and me. It was a tough neighborhood, but we managed. In a lot of ways we were the typical American family. For a few years, I guess, things were really good. I have vague memories of playing in the park with my mom. She usually let me push Amber in her stroller. I remember as Amber got older, that she and I would play on the kiddie swings. Mom and I took turns pushing her; she had to be no older than two.

I took the second Euclid exit off of I-71 and made the loop. As I pulled up to the stop sign, I noticed an old playground next to an elementary school that had seen better days. It had a tall, twisting slide with a tunnel, the kind the modern "kid-safe" playgrounds don't have. My hands began shaking and my chin quivered. Sun-Hi looked up.

"Are you okay, Greg?" she asked.

"I guess so," I replied, trying to regain composure.

I turned right after looking both ways at the stop sign, although there were no other cars in sight, just as it had been throughout the entire trip. Sun-Hi seemed fascinated with taking in all of the sights of Euclid. As I drove down the road leading into downtown, my mind was replaying scenes I hadn't thought of in years. I'd seen a slide like that before. It was a warm, summer day. There wasn't a cloud in the blue sky. It was one of those perfect, gorgeous days you read about in books. As I slowly drove the winding road into Euclid though, that unspeakable memory began to unfold once again.

***

"COME on, Mom," I yelled as Amber and I stood on the wooden porch in the front of our little house. "We're ready. Hurry up!"

"Hurry up!" Amber chimed in, imitating me.

My mother opened the screen door and locked the heavy oak door. She carried her purse and a basket that held morning snacks. She wore tan Capri pants and a light blue blouse. Her light brown hair was pulled back in a ponytail. She bounded off the front porch and took Amber's hand. I grabbed the basket. We were off to play at the park. It was the first day of summer and Amber and I were finally out of school. I'd finished up the third grade and Amber had just completed kindergarten. It had been a good school year. I made good grades and enjoyed almost everything about school. I'd been looking forward to summer, though. It was going to be fun. We'd do all kinds of things; Mom, Amber and me. We had big plans that we'd talked about for over a month. We'd go to museums, ball games, parks, carnivals and a ton of other really cool places. We were excited to start the summer with a play day in the park near our house.

It was already getting hot, though it was just mid-morning. I wore an "Indians" tee shirt and a pair of jean shorts. Amber had on blue plaid shorts and a yellow shirt. She also had a hat; a floppy yellow thing that was a cross between a sailor's hat and a fishing hat.

The park was only a half a mile or so from our house, so it was an easy walk. When we got there, we were even more excited. We were there before almost everyone else. Nearly the whole park was ours! A few kids were standing around the pond throwing bread to the ducks that swam in circles. Another couple of kids were bounding on the teeter-totters. No one was on the swings. A few parents sat on benches enjoying an early summer morning.

"Come on, Greg," Amber said as she pulled her hand from Mom's. "Push me on the swings."

I looked up at Mom who smiled at me.

"Go ahead, Greg," she said, "I'll make sure you get a turn. I'll take our stuff over to the bench right here. Be careful."

I nodded and grabbed Amber's hand. She practically pulled me to the swings and hopped up into the seat.

"Push me really high, okay," she asked, looking back at me.

"Okay," I told her. "Hang on."

I pulled her back as far as I could and pushed hard. She squealed as the swing began its ascent. I kept her swinging for about ten minutes when she got tired and asked me to help her stop. She let her sandals sweep the dirt under the swing to speed up her slowing down.

"That was fun," she said. "What's next?"

"I don't know," I replied as I noticed a maintenance man cutting the grass behind the shelter house with a push mower.

Amber made her choice clear by making a mad dash away from the swings toward the center of the playground.

"The spinning wheel," she exclaimed as she sprinted toward it.

"Amber," I told her as I caught up to her at the rusted wheel with the iron hand rails. "You always get sick on this."

"No I don't," she retorted. "Go real fast."

I took one of the rails and we began pushing the old wheel. It creaked and groaned a bit at first, but then it got going.

"On the count of three, jump on," I told Amber as we continued to push.

"Okay," she said, breathing heavily.

"One, two, three, jump!"

We jumped on and rode the spinning wheel for as long as it would turn.

"Well, you didn't get sick this time," I told her as it finally stopped.

"Nope, I never do. Let's do it again."

"Nah," I told her. "Let's go to the slide."

"I don't want to. It's too high."

"Come on. Don't be a chicken."

I took her hand and we walked to the slide. She wasn't nearly as excited about this as she had been about doing other things. We walked through the center of the park to the slide, which was right in front of the shelter house. Just behind the shelter house, the tree line indicated where the woods began. Signs marked different walking trails. I waved at Mom and pointed to the slide. She smiled and nodded. I tried to call out to her but my voice was drowned out by the noise of the mower. We finally came to the old giant slide.

"Okay Amber," I told her as she stared up at the imposing monster. "I'll be right behind you. You'll be okay."

Amber had pulled her yellow hat down over her ears, but she heard and had a quick reply.

"No way. I'm not going."

"Come on, Amber, it'll be fun. The slide's tall, but it's got a tunnel and a few curves; you'll love it."

"I'm not going," she replied defiantly as she crossed her arms.

"Okay," I told her. "Here's the deal. I'll go first and you watch. You'll see it is really fun. Then you go, okay?"

Amber lowered her arms and looked up at me.

"Okay, but you go first."

I smiled and began climbing the ladder.

"You'll see, Amber. It'll be great."

I got to the top of the ladder and it did seem pretty high. I could see Mom over by the bench. She was busy talking to another woman and didn't see me. I saw the kids by the pond and the few near the teeter-totters had moved to the spinning wheel. I looked down the slide and saw Amber. She stood at the end of slide, her yellow hat crooked on her head and her blond hair hanging loosely under her hat. Her blue shorts and yellow shirt stood out in colorful contrast to the grass and dirt around the slide. I saw the man behind the shelter house stop mowing and wipe his brow. He was looking at me and Amber. It was getting hot, all right.

"Okay, here goes."

I jumped into the slide. It was a wild ride. I tumbled and turned throughout the big slide and into the tunnel which seemed to last forever. It was a thrilling ride, especially for someone just out of third grade. I shouted, screamed and thought the world had been turned upside down for the entire twelve seconds it took to reach the end. I hurtled out of the end of the slide and crashed into the dirt at the base of it.

"Whoa, Amber," I called out. "Cool. It's your turn now. I told you…"

I stopped in mid-sentence. Amber wasn't standing there anymore. Her odd yellow hat was there, but Amber wasn't. I picked up her hat and stuffed it in my pocket and looked around. I didn't know what had happened. I never heard Amber say anything or yell, but I was in the slide, so I couldn't be sure. I saw the kids by the pond and the others at the spinning wheel. I noticed Mom was coming my way, but Amber wasn't with her. I saw the mower behind the shelter house, but the maintenance guy was gone. Mom came up to me quickly.

"Are you okay," she asked.

"I'm fine," I answered with tears starting to form in my eyes. "Where's Amber?"

Mom looked panicked.

"Isn't she right here with you?"

Mom and I ran throughout the playground calling for

Amber and begging her to come out. Other parents and kids helped, too. The police were contacted and they searched the whole area. Mom called Dad and he left the post office early. He spent hours looking around the entire area. Amber wasn't found that day and I hardly slept any that night. Mom and Dad didn't sleep at all. I just kept hoping that somehow Amber would show up on our front porch. I'd kept her goofy, yellow hat thinking she'd want it back when she came home. I kept looking for her to come running up the stairs to where our rooms were. She never did. Some police dogs found her later that next day. Her body was buried underneath some brush. The maintenance man was no maintenance man at all. He was arrested, tried and found guilty. They sentenced him to life in prison. From that point on, I'm guessing his life was a living hell, but I didn't think much more about him after the trial. Certainly the life he left my family was. My father was devastated and withdrew within himself. He drank, a lot. He lost his job at the post office and in less than a year after Amber's funeral, he left Mom and me. I didn't blame him, though. He was broken. Mom did her best to make things okay for her and me, but I never really saw her smile like I had on that last morning all of us were together. Something inside of her died the day Amber died. I knew it. For a long time, she blamed herself. She told me so. She went to all kinds of different counselors and tried to get me to go, too. I talked to quite a few. They never changed my mind, though. I knew who was responsible. It was my fault Amber got killed. I wish I'd never seen a slide like that.

***

"You know where you're going?" Sun-Hi interrupted my thoughts.

"Yeah, I guess I do," I told her.

I eased the jeep down an abandoned Main Street and tuned onto Flowers Boulevard. There it was. The old wood porch stood out in front of the house like an imposing sentinel guarding a treasure. The mailbox was still at the edge of the drive, just off the street.

"Is this it?" Sun-Hi asked.

"Yep," I answered. "This is where I grew up."

I sat in the jeep as Sun-Hi opened the door on her side and jumped down. She ran across the drive and jumped up on the sagging porch. It seemed like I should stop her from bothering whomever it was that lived there now, but I didn't have time. She stood at the door and knocked. I watched as the door creaked open and a figure appeared. I couldn't believe my eyes when I saw her. How could it be? She'd died five years ago. I knew she had. The Department of Corrections denied my request to go to the funeral. Though my brain was processing certain facts I knew to be true, my eyes were telling a different story. She stepped out onto the porch with Sun-Hi and back into my life. She looked older, weary, kind of beaten up by life, I guess. I opened the door of the jeep and climbed out. I rubbed my eyes and simply stared. She eased down off the porch and started walking toward me.

"Mom," I called out.

"Greg," she replied, "I'm so thankful. I knew you'd come."

Sun-Hi stood silently on the porch, watching, as Mom hugged me tightly.

"Come on in," she said as she led me up the steps of the porch and into the house.

"Mom," I started, "I'm not sure what's going on. I know this can't be happening, but then again, none of what's gone on so far *should* be happening."

"Greg, there are some clothes in the back bedroom. Change out of that awful orange suit. Then come and sit down at the table here. I've fixed breakfast."

I stood in the kitchen, the same one I knew when I was growing up here. Mom had Sun-Hi help her and they brought scrambled eggs and French toast to the table. Mom filled three plates and sat down at the table. I got us both a cup of coffee and Sun-Hi a glass of orange juice and sat down with them. I was still struggling to figure out what was happening. My mother died five years ago, yet here she was in our old house. It didn't make sense.

All I could do, for a while anyway, was eat. I hadn't had a meal like this for a long time. Mom broke the silence.

"Greg, we have some things to talk about and I'm afraid there's not much time."

"I guess so, Mom," I replied, though I wasn't sure what she meant about the "time" thing. Sun-Hi had mentioned that, too.

Mom put her fork down and dabbed the napkin to her lips.

"Greg, you understand by now, don't you, that what you're experiencing isn't of the 'real' world? You've been given a chance, before you die, to understand some things and to do something really important. I'm going to point you in the right direction. You have to choose, at that point, what you'll do."

I was famished for home cooking, but after hearing my mom, I lost interest in eating. What was that she said? I was no longer in the "real" world. I got that. I knew that right from the start. What was I supposed to understand and what could I possibly do that could be important?

"Mom," I started, "you seem to know more of what's going on than I do. What's happening? What should I do?"

Mom took a deep breath and exhaled slowly. Sun-Hi sat quietly in her chair, waiting. At last, Mom spoke.

"Greg, I know what you did with your life. You know that I hate it. I hate it with every fiber of my being. I can't help but blame myself, at least some."

I wanted to stop her right there. I wanted her to know that she wasn't at fault. Not at all. I was the one who got into stealing and drugs. I was the one who hung with thugs and crack-heads. I was the one who started using and selling. I was the one who brokered the bad deal. I was the one who pulled the trigger.

"Mom, wait. That's not…"

"Greg, there isn't time for that. I know you made the choices you made and I've come to terms with whatever part I played in it. That's not what this is about. You've already reaped what you've sown. I'm thinking you've figured that out by now. I'm also pretty sure that my little boy, the one who loved life, school, and his family is still in there, too, down deep inside. I think it was that little boy who called out for help when you were stabbed. The Lord heard your cry, Son. He still loves you. You'll meet him later today. However, in crying out like you did, he's giving you a chance that most don't get. You get a chance to fix some things, to make them right. Take Sun-Hi and go to Delhart, a town just south of Columbus. Look up a man named George Swisher. George will tell you what you need to do next. Please hurry."

My mind was racing. My mom knew all about what happened at the prison. She knew I was going to die, or that maybe I was already dead. I couldn't believe she knew these things. I was also puzzled by her instructions. I never knew any George Swisher and I'd never been to Delhart.

"Mom," I started, "hold on just a minute. You gotta tell me some more. This is crazy. How do you know all these things? Who is this Swisher? You even seem to know Sun-Hi, how?"

"Greg, you just have to trust. Please go. Do as I told you."

She stood and took Sun-Hi by the hand and began walking to the door.

"Go, Greg."

Reluctantly, I got up from the table. There would be no more answers. Not here, anyway.

"Okay, Mom," I said to her as I took Sun-Hi's hand. "We'll go."

As I began to walk slowly out onto the porch, Mom grabbed me and hugged me tightly.

"Greg, don't forget I love you. I'll be seeing you, Son."

She let me go and Sun-Hi and I walked back to the Jeep. I opened her door and she climbed in. I walked around the back of the Jeep and opened the door to get in. I looked back to the porch for a final wave to Mom. I was stunned! The house was boarded up. There was broken glass lying all around a dilapidated porch. No one was standing there or had been standing there for a long time.

Chapter Three

A warm, early summer sun was just beginning to rise in the small town of Delhart. Delhart, or "Round Town" as it was once known, had a special place in the state's history books. Founded in the mid 1800's, Delhart had been a booming metropolis at the turn of the century. The layout of the town itself added to its charm. The town was arranged in a unique manner. The main parts of the city, the courthouse and a cluster of shops, were constructed first. The rest of the town was built in a circular manner around that hub; Round Town. It was built near the river, so in the early years it had been a thriving manufacturing and farming hub. Canals were built to enhance financial opportunities. Delhart was the place to be in those early years.

As the century changed, so did Delhart. The advent of trucking changed shipping and remade Delhart. The canals were still there, but the big thrust was in factories. Delhart saw two big ones arrive. A nationally known paint company made Delhart its headquarters. They built several houses and neighborhoods for workers. These became known as the "Paint District." The second was a grocer that moved to Delhart and operated a regional distribution center. Population increased and it looked like Delhart might see some really significant growth. Throughout two world wars, Delhart was thriving. After the Second World War, though, things began to change again. The paint company found a place in the south where taxes were less and moved. In its place came a television tube factory. Workers continued to work and live in the "Paint District" as they made television tubes instead of paint. In the late 1960's the grocer had to consolidate, so the center in Delhart closed. The building remained empty for several years until it was converted into a Wal-Mart. The once thriving town was now on the decline and young people were leaving the community at a higher rate than those who were moving in. In the nineties, the tech revolution dealt a blow to Delhart. No one needed television tubes anymore, so the factory closed. This time, nothing came in its place. The "Paint District" remained but factory workers no longer lived there. It became low-income housing. The town changed, too. It became "harder." There were some really fine areas in which many people lived. Some family names were still prominent. There were good schools, churches and neighborhoods. However, a different Delhart also existed. It was a more dangerous Delhart; a place where drugs could be bought, robbery and flaunting the law were common, and murder was as ordinary as the church bells ringing at noon. No one talked much about this Delhart, but it was there.

***

I⊤ was in that Delhart that Sara emerged from her trailer. The trailer park was in the south part of town, a place near the state juvenile correctional facility. She yawned and stretched. Sara was celebrating her thirty-second birthday in just two days, but she didn't look it. Tending bar and running the grill at Danny's had taken its toll. That and an addiction to meth had left her looking at least ten years older. The bright June sun hurt her eyes, so she donned sunglasses as she climbed into her green Ford Ranger. She turned the key in the ignition and revved the engine. She backed out of the gravel drive and maneuvered out onto the access road in front of the run-down trailer park. In minutes she was out on the highway and headed toward the south part of town. She had an important meeting today; a business meeting. It had nothing to do with Danny's. It was bigger than that. She pulled off the highway into the parking lot of an abandoned car wash. She took off the glasses and looked herself over in the rear view mirror. She saw the dark circles under her eyes and her gaunt, pale complexion. A rash was starting to spread on her neck. She swore. She knew she wasn't in the best of health and she promised herself that she would do better.

A Chevy truck pulled into the run-down parking lot. A tall, slender man sauntered his way out of the truck. He wore a stiff, wine colored collared shirt and new blue jeans. His black hair was combed back and sunglasses framed his tanned face. Michael Calento had arrived.

"Hey Sara," he said as he approached her truck, "I got what you ordered. You need anything else?"

Sara rolled down her window and gave a small leather

bag to Michael.

"Here's the down payment. I'll leave the rest for you at the pick-up spot."

"Okay," Michael replied, "you'll need to go to the strip mall where the video store used to be. Manny will meet you there. You don't have to find him. He'll find you. Give him the cash and he'll give you the stash. Pretty simple."

Sara nodded.

"Be there in an hour. You understand?"

"Yes," Sara replied, "I understand."

It was just that simple. Sara gave him five thousand as a down payment with another seven to be exchanged with Manny. She would get twelve ounces of cocaine. She had used her share of drugs. She'd smoked marijuana and was quite adept at making meth. Straight cocaine, though, she never used that stuff. She sold it, though, all throughout Ohio. Business was business and right now business was good. This deal would set her up for a long time.

Sara watched as Michael pulled away from the parking lot. The whole transaction had taken place right out in the open, just off the main highway headed south out of town. It had taken less than three minutes and no one seemed to notice. No one cared.

Sara drove her truck back onto the highway. She had an hour until she'd meet Manny. Almost without thinking, she found herself in the parking lot of the tire shop. She got out, wondering if George was in. She had time for a quick visit.

The air was heavy with the smell of grease and rubber.

"Swisher Tires" had been a part of the business community in Delhart for years. Generations of Swishers had rolled tires, strong-armed jacks and equipped the cars of this town for as long as anyone could remember. The shop was now being run by a Swisher named Grant. As Sara got out of the truck, she noticed Grant talking with the pastor of the local Baptist church about new tires for the church van. She waved. He acknowledged her and pointed to the back as the pastor continued to talk. She maneuvered her way past Nancy's desk. Nancy was Grant's wife and the bookkeeper and secretary here. She passed the stacks of old tires and dodged the ancient grease spots on the garage floor on her way to the tiny office in the back of the shop.

"Hey old man," she called out as she entered through the door. "What are you up to on this fine day?"

A portly man with snow-white hair was seated in the creaking rolling chair. He looked up from the tire magazine he was perusing and over his reading glasses to see just who had interrupted his solitude. When he saw Sara, he smiled broadly and stood. His belly lapped over his belt as he pushed the chair away from the desk and moved toward her.

"Sara, how are you?" he exclaimed as he swallowed her in a bear hug. "You never said anything about coming by today, what's going on?"

Sara pulled out of his embrace just a bit.

"There's not much going on, George," she started.

George, though, looked her over and into her dark glasses.

"Uh huh," he answered, unconvinced.

"You're still as skinny as a rail," he told her as he pulled her away from the desk and to the door of the tiny office. "I'm worried about you. You're losing too much weight."

"Well, I guess we should switch eating habits," Sara retorted as she patted George's ample belly. "You're as big as ever."

She winked at him.

"I suppose you're right on that," George answered. "Sara, I am worried about you though. You sure you're okay? You don't look so good, kid. You're not still..."

Before he could finish, Sara cut him off.

"George, you know I'm fine. You know that I'm not doing that junk anymore. I told you that. Can't I visit my favorite customer from Danny's without getting the third degree?"

George put his big hand on her shoulder.

"Okay, Sara. I'm just concerned that's all."

"I know, George," Sara replied as she hugged him.

As George broke free from her embrace, he exclaimed, "Hey, your birthday's coming up. Me and the missus, we have something for you. Can we bring it by tonight?"

Sara smiled as they walked out of the office toward the front of the garage.

"You all are so nice to me. You don't have to..."

"Nonsense! We want to. We'll come by Danny's right after church tonight. Hey, you wanna come? You said you would sometime."

"I will sometime, George, but not tonight. I've got another appointment. I'll have the grill nice and hot for you, though, when you come after church."

George smiled and waved to her as he made his way back to the little office. Sara paused to watch him as he ambled back there. She'd thought it before, but now it was even more apparent. The old man loved her. He and his wife cared. She slipped by the grease and waved good-bye to George's son Grant and his wife Nancy. As she got into the truck and turned the ignition, her mind continued to race. *He and the missus got her a birthday present! Unbelievable.* She doubted whether anyone else would even know her birthday was coming. She'd do something nice for George and his wife. Maybe she'd even go to church with them. Sunday might work. *Yeah, I'll check with them tonight.*

***

GEORGE got back to the office his daddy and his daddy's daddy had used to run this old place. The rolling chair groaned as he plopped his girth back into it. He didn't pick up the trade magazine, though. He was troubled. George was a Christian. He didn't really go in for all the flashy stuff, he just tried to live his life the way the Good Book prescribed. He prayed, loved his wife, tried to do his best by his family and run a good, honest business. He and his wife Frances had lived in this town for over sixty years. They'd raised Grant and his sister Grace here. Grant had taken over the business several years ago. It was a tribute to the kind of man Grant was that he insisted George keep the office. George had been a good, solid fellow. He and Frances had been members of the Community Church of Delhart since its founding. He was thought of as a kind, outgoing, generous, happy man.

As he sat at the ancient desk, though, he was bothered.

Lord, I don't know what it is, but something's not right with Sara. Please, Lord. Use someone or something to reach her.

George's prayers were hardly ever audible to anyone on this earth, but his heart cried out to heaven. Tears filled his eyes as he thought more about Sara. She'd been in town for less than ten years. She'd lived a wild life and George and Frances could tell right away that her road had been rocky. They met her on her first night at Danny's.

✳✳✳

THE couple came in as if they'd owned the place. He had tufts of snow-white hair and a heavy blue windbreaker which struggled to contain a prodigious belly. She came in holding his hand. That seemed odd to Sara, but no one else seemed to notice. They joked with Danny and then took an empty table in Sara's section. As Sara approached them with menus, the old guy, George spoke.

"Hey kid, you're new here, aren't you?"

"Yes sir," Sara replied. "This is my first night. May I give you a menu and get you drinks?"

"Well," George said as he leaned back in his chair. "We won't need any menus, but we'll have two iced teas, unsweetened. We're also ready to order when you're ready for it."

"All right, sir," Sara replied, "I'll have those teas out to you. Now what can I get for you and your daughter?"

Frances laughed and George reared back in mock surprise.

"You need some help, young lady, if you think this is my daughter!"

"George, leave the girl alone. Obviously, she is perceptive and wise beyond her years. I'll have the grilled chicken sandwich and he'll have the wing plate as he always does."

"Sauce on the side," George added.

Immediately Sara brought the drinks and shortly after, she brought in the food. She had placed the sauce on the side, just as George had requested. She even brought extra napkins and tucked one under his collar.

"Don't want to mess up that nice, clean shirt."

The good-natured banter continued and George laughed loudly and a lot.

As they left that night, Frances and George had been impressed.

"You'll do just fine here, young lady. You have a great spirit, Miss, uh…"

"Call me Sara, please."

"Okay, Sara it is. We're here four or five times a week. We'll be checking in on you."

Sara smiled.

"Great. I'll have the wings ready to go."

✳ ✳ ✳

OVER the next ten years George and Frances got to know Sara even better. They knew she'd come from the northern part of the state. They knew she had little or no family. She rarely, if ever, said a word about any kin. She'd advanced at Danny's and they'd celebrated her success. They even had her over for Thanksgiving one year. They also knew about Sara's "tough" side. She'd told them about her battles with drugs. She'd confided in them, like they were her grandparents, about her temptations and struggles. They loved her and showed that love as freely and as often as she would let them. There had been a time, three or four years in a row, where Sara had been clean. She'd met a guy and even talked about going to church with them. That time, though, seemed but a distant memory. In the last year or so, she'd regressed.

She'd never admit it, but they knew she was back on drugs and doing who knows what. They'd tried to approach her, but she remained distant. As George put his head down on the old desk, his heart was nearly broken. He rested his head on that desk and continued to pray for Sara.

Chapter Four

Her truck sprayed gravel as she pulled away from the parking lot at Swisher's Tire. Sara enjoyed her short visit with George, but she couldn't stay there long. She had a meeting to attend. She sped down Arcadia Street much faster than the posted speed limit. After stopping at the light, she turned onto Main. In just a few minutes she pulled into the lot surrounding what used to be a video rental place. It was almost noon and people were milling about, seeking a quick lunch and a few minutes to enjoy a warm, summer day. Sara slid down in her seat, almost as if she didn't want to be seen. No one was paying any attention to her, but she felt self-conscious. *Where was Manny!* She glanced at her watch. He was already five minutes late. She'd just decided to leave when she saw the van turn into the abandoned lot. The beat-up, old van rolled to a stop in the gravel right next to her Ranger. In just seconds, a man stepped out. He wore a white painter's shirt and wrinkled gray work pants. He carried a small money bag. A ball cap was perched on his head and sunglasses framed his face. At last, Manny appeared.

He approached her window and motioned for her to lower it. Sara was certain everyone on the street was gawking, but the truth was, not many even noticed the two of them in the desolate lot.

"Hey," Manny said as the window opened. "Michael said you'd be here. I got what you want. You got the money?"

Sara winced as she heard him speak. Was she really dealing with these two thugs? She couldn't help but think of her conversation with George just an hour or so ago. What did it matter? She was in business with these two and that was that.

"Yeah," she replied, "I got it."

"Good," Manny answered and smiled, flashing his yellow teeth.

Sara took out the small bag and passed it over to Manny. He took it and gave her the money bag. In a matter of seconds, he was back in the van and backing out of the lot. Sara sat in the Ranger for a few minutes. Though she now had more cocaine than before and an additional bag of money that Manny didn't know about, she wasn't nervous anymore about being found out. Everyone was absorbed in their own lives and no one noticed the transaction that had taken place, almost no one. Behind the convenience store, across Main Street, two men sat in an old Ford. Though they said nothing, they plainly saw what went down in the parking lot. Sara took a deep breath and relaxed a bit. She eased the truck out of the old lot and back onto Main. As she did, the man driving the Ford started its engine. Sara had a few hours before she had to be at Danny's and wanted to take care of business. She didn't want this stash in her possession very long. She'd get out to the Willard place, make the delivery and get back to Danny's for her night shift. She turned onto Lancaster Pike and gunned the engine. The Ranger responded and in a few minutes she was miles out of town. About a quarter of a mile back or so, an old Ford followed.

✳ ✳ ✳

THE morning had been busy at Swisher Tire. Grant checked out one car after another, not to mention the church van that was brought in. It seemed like everyone needed tires all at once. They didn't even get a break for lunch. He hadn't seen "Pop" for quite some time, so when there was a bit of a lull in the hectic pace of the day, he set out to check on him.

"Hey Nancy," he called out, "did you see Pop leave?"

"No," she replied, looking up from the stacks of paper. "I know he was in the back earlier, but I haven't seen him in quite a while. Maybe he slipped out for lunch."

Grant wove his way around the stacks of tires and dodged the grease spots. He pushed the office door and it creaked open.

"Hey Pop," he called out, "you back there? If so, you gotta get going. Mom's gonna be mad if you're late getting home."

George's head never left the desk. It never moved. Grant went to shake him, "Wake up. You gotta get going. Mom will want to meet you pretty quick."

George wasn't moving. Grant reached out to wake him, but he wasn't waking up.

"Oh no, it can't be. Please, God. Nancy! Call 911!"

The paramedics arrived and so did Frances and Grace. Grant held his mom as they loaded George onto the gurney and into the ambulance. Nancy and Grace stood, shocked and silent. They closed the shop early and followed the ambulance. The paramedics rushed George into the Emergency Room. There was a frantic rush and people were moving fast and machines were beeping. It all seemed surreal as the four of them stood in the corner of the waiting room. A young doctor appeared after a few minutes. He spoke and Frances wilted when he told her George was dead.

***

THE trip from Euclid to Delhart should've taken nearly three hours, but Sun-Hi and I traveled the abandoned highway in virtually no time at all. Neither of us said much on the trip. Sun-Hi was content to take in the bright, blue sky and the green grass along the highway. I, however, was anything but content. In my mind I replayed the events of this morning. Was I already dead and in an alternate state? How could I see my mom for a while and then have her disappear as if she had never been there? As I continued to dwell on all of these things, one thought kept coming to the surface. *Where is everyone? Why am I only seeing people who aren't there?* I turned to look at Sun-Hi who was admiring a cloud formation. *Except for her; she seems to be real.* I turned off Highway 71 and eased the Jeep onto the state highway that led into Delhart. As we passed by an old, abandoned barn, I turned to Sun-Hi.

"Where do you think we should go to find this George

Swisher?"

I felt a bit awkward asking a twelve year old a serious question like that, but what else was there to do? Sun-Hi turned away from the window and looked at me.

"Why don't we just drive around town and maybe something will come up."

That seemed to be as good an idea as any, so I drove the Jeep down the empty highway. As we approached the town we noticed the feed store, several churches and a dentist office. What we didn't see were people. We came to the stop light at the center of Delhart and turned left toward the downtown area.

"We'll go downtown and see if we can find anyone who knows George Swisher," I told Sun-Hi as we stopped at another light. There wasn't another car in sight, but the lights were working.

"Why don't we try there?" Sun-Hi said as she pointed to a convenience store.

"All right. We might as well see what we can."

We got out of the Jeep and walked around the store. There was no one at the gas pumps or in the store. It looked like the store was open; the door was unlocked and stuff was on the shelves, but there wasn't a soul in sight.

"Hello," I called out, "is anyone here?"

I walked to the rear of the store, but didn't find any-one. Sun-Hi was standing and staring at a bulletin board on the wall of the store.

"Hey Greg," she said, "come here."

I walked up to the bulletin board to see what had cap-tured Sun-Hi's attention.

"Look."

Sun-Hi pointed to a faded yellow sheet on the board advertising a sale on tires. It was at Swisher Tires.

"I think that's him," she said.

"It won't hurt to find out. Copy the address and we'll check it out."

✳ ✳ ✳

SARA always had a lead foot, but she drove faster than usual down Lancaster Pike. The beat-up Ford struggled to keep up with the streaking Ranger. Sara's mind, though, wasn't on her driving. *If I can just make this deal; deliver this package; get the money, I'll get out of this business. George and Frances are right. I've got to change my life. Just one more deal. This is it.* Her thoughts were broken up by the beeping of her cell phone. She pulled it out of her purse and glanced quickly at the number. It was Danny's. *Why would someone at Danny's be calling me?* Her curiosity got the better of her and she quickly pulled off Lancaster and onto state road AA. She drove just a bit down the road and stopped the truck. The driver of the Ford didn't notice her on AA and continued down Lancaster Pike. She quickly pushed the call back button.

"Hey Danny, what's up? You called? I'm not supposed to be in until five."

"Yeah," Danny replied, "I know. I just got a call though that I thought you needed to know about."

"What is it?" Sara answered.

Danny hesitated.

"Why don't you just come in? I'd rather talk to you in person."

"Can't right now; come on, just tell me. What is it?"

"Okay. Uh, just got a call from a guy I know at the hospital. He told me that George Swisher was rushed in this afternoon. Sara, he didn't make it. I thought you should know."

There was a pause.

"Hey, you okay? I know it's a shock."

Sara composed herself to speak.

"Yeah Danny, thanks for telling me."

"You want tonight off? I know you all were pretty close."

"No, I'll be there."

Sara hung up and put her hands to her face. It had been a long time since she'd really cried, but the tears came freely. After a few minutes, she started the Ranger and drove back onto Lancaster Pike. She'd forget about going to the Willard place for now. She knew where she wanted to go.

***

I took the address from Sun-Hi and we got into the Jeep. Together we programmed the address into the GPS and it didn't take long for us to be back out on Main Street. It seemed like it should be just after noon, but no one was in town. It felt weird driving in an empty town, but this whole experience had been weird.

"We're not too far away," I said to Sun-Hi as we turned off of Arcadia. "It should be right down this street."

Sun-Hi saw the sign before I did.

"Greg, look," she said, pointing to the sign that said "Swisher Tires."

There weren't any cars in the lot, which I thought had

to be a bad sign for business. I pulled the Jeep right up next to the building and we both got out. Sun-Hi rushed around the Jeep and took my hand as we walked to the door. The garage doors were shut and it looked like the place was closed. I pushed on the front door and a bell rang as it opened. The front desk was empty. We moved past it and into the garage where there were a few cars and some tires stacked in random places. A few grease spots dotted the concrete floor.

"Hey," I called out. "Are you open? Is anyone here?"

There was a noise in a back office. The door started to open. A man was shuffling toward us. He smiled and I noticed his snowy white hair and large belly.

"Good to see ya," he called out to us as he extended his hand.

I shook his hand.

"We're looking for George Swisher. Do you know him?"

"Well, you came to the right place. You just met him."

***

Sara's vision was blurred by tears as she drove back down Lancaster Pike. She turned onto Mill Creek Road and headed out to a spot she knew very well. *How could George be gone, just like that? It can't be. It has to be a mistake. I just saw him!* She passed the entrance to Briar Wood State Park and instinctively drove to Shelter House B. She pulled the Ranger up the winding gravel road and stopped next to the pavilion. Trees outlined the little shelter house, giving it a sense of privacy. Sara stepped out of the truck and walked the path behind the shelter and down the hill to Mill Creek. As she sat on a stump and watched the water flow, memories flooded her mind.

George and Frances had introduced her to this place. Their Sunday school class held a picnic out here every year. Sara hadn't wanted to go and had put them off for a few years. They persisted and she finally gave in. She was thankful she did. That first picnic was a little weird. She'd driven out by herself and arrived a few minutes late. Even though Frances told her she didn't need to bring anything, she'd brought macaroni salad. As she drove up that gravel path off of Mill Creek Road, the cars were lined up along the side. The sky had clouded over and turned gray. It wasn't long after she'd arrived that the sky opened up and a loud thunder storm rumbled through Briar Wood. The crowd of people that had been milling around the shelter now huddled inside. People got really close. George later joked with her that was the Lord's way of getting her to meet people. George and Frances hoped that she might start attending church with them. That never became a priority for her, but many times after that first stormy gathering she met the Swishers and others at Shelter House B. It was a hidden place of contentment and peace for her.

Now, though, as she sat next to the creek, she wrestled with the difficult fact that George was gone. He wouldn't be at the shop. He and Frances wouldn't be coming into Danny's, ordering wings and teasing about some silly little thing. He wouldn't nag her about going to church anymore. He was really gone. Sara had never felt more alone.

***

I was surprised to see George Swisher standing right in front of me. When Sun-Hi and I drove into Delhart, I had no idea how we'd find the George Swisher my mom mentioned before she disappeared. It was incredible that the only person we met in Delhart was George Swisher!

"What can I do for you two?" George asked, smiling. "You have tire troubles?"

"No, not really," I answered. "I don't know. Uh," I stammered.

How do you tell a complete stranger that you're in his shop because your mother, who is no longer living, told you to come to this town to which you'd never been and find him?

"You two look a bit tired," George interjected. "Why don't you come back to my office and we'll sit for a bit; figure out what this is all about."

Sun-Hi and I followed George to the back office. He plopped down in the swivel chair behind the desk. Sun-Hi and I took the two chairs in front of the desk.

"You thirsty, kiddo?" he asked Sun-Hi. "Here," he said reaching to a cooler under the desk. "I always keep a stash of sodas under here."

He passed one to her and opened one for himself.

"You want one?" he asked me.

"No thanks. I just need to…"

"I know why you're here, Greg. You're here about Sara."

I was shocked. How did this guy know who I was! Who was this Sara?

"Wait," I shot back. "How do you know who I am?"

"Come on, Greg," the old man replied. "You know what happened this morning and you saw your mother just a bit ago. I'm here to point out what to do next."

I struggled to grasp what this old fellow was saying, but somehow what he was saying made sense. It did seem like I was on a mission. From the time I met Sun-Hi, then Mom and now here; it had all been a journey. Where it led I wasn't sure. I was going with it, though. What else could I do?

"You've been given a chance to do something right, Greg. Sun-Hi told you that earlier. Your mom directed you here. Now it's my turn."

"You said something about Sara. Who is that?"

George leaned back in the old swivel chair, so much so that it almost collapsed.

"One of the sweetest, kindest young ladies you'll ever meet."

"Okay, so what about this Sara? Who is she? What does she have to do with me?"

George leaned forward in the chair, crashing his belly on the desk.

"Greg, this is the important part. This is your chance to do something right before you're done."

"Okay," I replied, "I get that. But who is she? What does this Sara have to do with me?"

George took a deep breath and exhaled.

"Greg, you did a lot of things before you were sent to prison - petty crimes, gang activities, drugs."

It might have been strange, at one point, for this perfect stranger to know so much about my past, but I'd accepted that this was strange earlier today.

"You had plenty of young ladies, too."

I nodded, unsure of where this was going.

"Greg, one of those young ladies had a baby. The momma did her best, I suppose, but she couldn't raise a kid alone. She was really a kid herself. When the child was just a toddler, her momma gave her up. The momma's got her own story, but the kid was in and out of foster care for the rest of her childhood."

At this point, I was following every word. My mind was racing. Was this old man going to say what I thought he was going to say?

"Greg, Sara's that child. She's your daughter and she's in trouble."

It seemed like he wanted to continue, but I was stuck on the word *daughter.* It was unbelievable, but instinctively, I knew it was true. I had a daughter!

"George, where is she?"

"I'm not sure, but I've got a good guess. Briar Wood State Park, there's a shelter house there, Shelter House B."

"Where is Briar Wood Park, George?"

"Out past Lancaster Pike, but…"

I didn't wait to hear any more. I jumped up from the chair.

"Hold on," George called out. "There's more…"

I wasn't about to wait. I stood quickly and grabbed Sun-Hi's hand.

"Come on, Sun-Hi. I know where we're going this time."

Chapter Five

The two men in the old Ford were frustrated as they drove up and down Lancaster Pike looking for the Ford Ranger that had somehow disappeared. They turned down several country roads and county highways, but saw no sign of the Ranger. It was beginning to wear on them.

"How could we lose her?" the younger of the two asked the driver. "If we don't find her and get there when the deal goes down, people are going to be furious."

"Don't you think I know that," the driver snarled. "We'll make a couple more trips over this road to make sure we didn't miss her turning off. Maybe she went to that bar and grill, Danny's. I don't know. We know she's not at the Willard place yet, but she'll end up there sometime today. The informant has already made that clear. We just have to be there when she does. Call in and tell them we're still looking. We'll find her. We always do. As soon as we have something, we'll let them know."

The younger man phoned in the message and they continued to slowly drive down Lancaster Pike, looking for a green Ford Ranger.

✷ ✷ ✷

THE water continued to flow down Mill Creek. Sara sat on a nearby rock, watching the water and listening to the crickets, birds and an occasional bull frog. The scene around her was one of peace and tranquility, but it only masked the pain and hurting that consumed her. The sounds of nature were interrupted by the blaring of her cell phone. Sara sighed and looked at the caller ID.

Michael? Why would he be calling?

"Hello."

"Sara, this is Michael. Can you talk?"

"Yeah, I guess so," she replied. "What's up?"

"Hey, you haven't been to the Willard place yet, have you?"

"No."

"Good. Listen. Things have changed a bit. Got a text from a guy down south. I'm bringing more than what I gave you. We make the deal there and then we're set for life. No more nickel and dime junk. We'll be in a big chain, making big cash. You bring what I gave you and I'll bring the rest. Hey, you know I didn't have to cut you in on this. Some of the guys wanted to leave you out, but you've been really good, and I didn't want to see you left out of the big score. So, you in girl or what?"

Sara heard what Michael said but it was taking a while to register.

"Hey, you hear me? Are you in or what?"

She already had some reservations about the deal she'd set up. Now it had gotten bigger, more danger-ous, but more lucrative. She had wanted to get out of this lifestyle. Do something else. Live a real life. She thought about George and Frances, maybe even a little about God, whom they talked about all of the time. But George was dead. Where was God in that?

"Sorry. Yeah. I'm in. I'll be there."

"Good. We'll meet at six."

"I'm supposed to work at Danny's tonight."

"Skip it. You won't need that anymore. It's the big time, baby. See you. Don't be late."

"Got it."

✳ ✳ ✳

Sun-Hi and I practically ran out of the tire shop. George tried several times to get us to slow down; to wait. I couldn't do it, though. For the first time in this whole weird situation, I felt in control. I had a daughter that I didn't know I had. That's a shock, but hearing that someone is in trouble and knowing that you're in that particular place for that particular moment, gives a sense of clarity. At least it did for me. I threw open the door of the Jeep for Sun-Hi and ran around to the other side. George had shuffled to the edge of the garage.

"Hold on a minute, Greg. Stop."

"Can't. I know what I need to do!"

I jumped in, slammed the door and started the Jeep. I backed out of the empty lot around Swisher's and got back on Arcadia. I was headed to Lancaster Pike. I'd seen a sign for that when we were in town. I was driving much faster than the posted limits, but there wasn't anyone around. As we pulled out onto Lancaster Pike toward Briar Wood, it occurred to me that Sara might not be able to interact with me.

"Sun-Hi, so far we've only seen people who, well, weren't really there; Mom and George. Do you think Sara will be able to see me? Do you think I'll be able to talk to her?"

Sun-Hi looked up at me as I drove. She had a look of concern, as if she had thought of this, too.

"I don't know, Greg," she answered. "I'm not sure. Do you think we should've waited to hear more of what George was trying to say?"

I had thought that, too, for a fleeting instant. I didn't want to let on to Sun-Hi, though, that I had any hesitation.

"No. I'm sure this is right. I can feel it."

"Okay," she replied, but her face bore a shadow of doubt.

✳✳✳

THE men in the old Ford drove back into Delhart and parked behind the convenience store as they had before. They would simply wait. She'd show up again and they'd get out to the Willard place just after six. One of them, the driver, pulled out a cigarette.

"Hey, don't you know smoking's bad for you?" his partner asked.

"Yeah, but so is what we do. Besides, this is a habit that I've had for forty years. Why stop now?"

"Did you hear about that race down at Bristol? Wasn't that something?"

Their light-hearted banter was broken up by the buzzing of a cell phone.

"Who could that be?" the younger of the two asked.

"I don't know. What does it say?"

"It's from Daniels."

"Better answer it."

The younger of the two spoke on the phone for a bit. He ended the conversation and looked to his senior partner.

"Well, it's gotten bigger."

"Oh, in what way?"

"Daniels said they got word that this is the biggest one in the state so far. Some really heavy hitters are going to be there tonight. Lots of money on the table. Big time."

His partner smiled.

"We'll be there."

***

Sara put her phone back in her purse. She looked at the creek; the water cascading over the rocks. A small voice in her mind struggled to be heard.

Don't do it, Sara. You can do so much better; so much more. Throw the bag away and go to Danny's. Never talk to Michael, Manny or anyone else like them again.

The voice presented a good case. Sara hesitated. She could just leave. It might work. At last she stood to go back to the Ranger. Leaving wasn't an option. Where could she go? She needed cash. This deal would set her up for life. The thoughts of completing the deal were gaining strength. *This is it, though. This is the last time.* Her thoughts were broken by the crunch of gravel next to the shelter. Someone else had stopped by Shelter House B.

✳ ✳ ✳

I PUT all negative thoughts out of my mind. I smiled at Sun-Hi. *Sure she'll be able to see me. I'll be able to talk to her. This is what this whole thing is about. My life is over, but I get a chance to meet and help my daughter. That's the important thing I have to do.*

"We're almost to the park," Sun-Hi said as we turned off Lancaster Pike and onto Mill Creek Road.

"Yep, we are."

I turned the Jeep at the entrance of Briar Wood State Park and began checking the signs for Shelter House B. After a few miles of winding, wooded roads, a sign indicated Shelter House B and pointed to a narrow, gravel road. In the distance I saw a green Ford Ranger parked next to the shelter. The gravel crunched and skidded as I parked the Jeep a few spaces away from the Ranger. As I got out, I could hear the splashing of the water in the creek down the hill. Sun-Hi walked around the Jeep, stood next to me and we just listened. I was lost in the beauty of the scene around me. Sun-Hi saw her first. She tugged my hand.

"Greg, there she is. Do you see her?"

I looked. Coming up the path from the creek was a young lady wearing jeans, a loose fitting white top and sun glasses; I could see Sara.

I wasn't sure what to say; what do you say to a daughter you've never met? She saw me and Sun-Hi and she spoke first.

"Hey, sorry. I didn't mean to take up space in the shelter. I don't have it reserved. I'm leaving now. You can have it."

She ran her hands through her hair and then reached into her purse to get her keys.

"Wait," I started, "You don't have to leave yet. We don't have a reservation for this shelter either."

"Oh, that's okay," she replied, getting her keys, "I have to go anyway."

She started to walk away. I couldn't just let her go. This wasn't how it was supposed to be.

"Sara, wait a minute."

She stopped and turned to face me. She frowned.

"How do you know my name? I don't know you. Did Michael send you to check on me? You should know I carry a gun and know how to use it. You come at me in any sort of awkward way, and it'll be the last move you make."

I winced. It was pretty clear from the way Sara talked and the things she did that she was my daughter.

Sun-Hi backed away a bit and sat down on a bench in the shelter. I raised both hands.

"No, it isn't anything like that. I don't know what you're hiding or why you'd need a gun, but I'm not here for any of that."

"Uh huh," she said as she eyed me warily. "Then what do you want? Who are you?"

This was it. It was time for the truth. I felt sure that somewhere my mother had prayed for this moment.

"Can we sit down a minute? Do you mind?"

"I think I'd like to know who you are before I sit with you."

"Fair enough. My name is Greg McBride. You don't know me and I don't know you, but I feel certain we were supposed to meet."

"Is this about the deal tonight? If so, I already heard from Michael. I'm set. I only talk with him and his people. You know Michael?"

I figured I was in this far with the truth, so I should just go with it.

"No, I don't."

"Then I don't have time to waste sitting with you. Later."

She started toward the Ranger again.

"Wait, please. You don't have to sit, but hear me out for a few minutes. Please. You can spare a couple of minutes, right?"

"All right. You got two minutes. What is so important that you have to interrupt me here?"

I took a deep breath.

"Sara, may I ask you a few questions?"

"Go ahead."

"Do you remember anything about your family?"

"No, I don't. I had a mom but she gave me up when I was barely three. I heard later that she'd been killed in a gang fight. I never knew for sure why she gave me up, but I kind of get it now. It had to be tough, just her and me. I guess she couldn't take care of me. Her life had to be pretty hard. She got killed and all. I spent most of my childhood in one foster family after another. Some were good. Some weren't. I survived."

"What about a father? Did you ever know about or think about your dad?"

Sara laughed derisively.

"Yeah, right. A few of the foster dads were okay, but

I never knew the loser who was there at the time of my conception. He had no time for my mom and, as far as I know, never knew I existed. So no, I never thought about him. I never needed him. Never will."

I took a deep breath. This was getting much harder than I thought and nothing at all like the dramatic, happy ending of a movie.

"Uh, yeah, I can see where you're coming from. My dad left me when I was young, too. I get the anger."

"So what, your time is running out."

"Okay, here it is. This is going to sound weird, but hear me out. This morning I was in prison, doing life for killing a guy. I was double-crossed and stabbed. Before I died, I prayed."

I glanced at Sun-Hi and continued, "This little girl showed up and has taken me to a couple of places I thought I'd never go again. I just found out that you exist. I think I'm supposed to help you. Hey, I know it's really late, right? But here goes. Truth. Sara, I'm your father."

Her eyes were hidden behind the sun glasses. She curled her lip and smirked.

"What drugs are you on? Talk about hallucinations!"

"No Sara. Really. It's true. We've been on a journey. I don't know why or how to explain it, but you're a part of it. Tell me what's going on. Let me try to help."

Her smirk turned to an angry snort. She yanked off the sun glasses.

"Really? You want to try to help? So, you're my *Daddy* showing up at the last minute to save the day? Wow! You're here to help, huh? Said you were in prison this morning. Sounds like you're the one who needs help!"

She paused for a moment to reflect on this newly discovered truth.

"Hearing how your life's been, you sound like the kind of guy I'd get for a dad. So, *Dad,* you've finally come to help, huh? Where were you when Momma and I were struggling in that rat-infested apartment? Where were you?"

As she ranted, the scenes formed in my mind. I didn't want to see them, but they were there.

❄❄❄

It was a small apartment in downtown Cleveland. There were some good apartment buildings there and some nice neighborhoods. This wasn't one of them. There wasn't much furniture for a living room, bedroom and bathroom. A mother and her child lived here. They both slept in the same bed. The night sky could be seen through the one window which had no curtain or blind. Street lights were the night light for this little home.

"Come on, baby. Go to sleep. Momma needs her rest, too."

The little girl in the bed, however, was wide awake. She wanted to play. Her momma, not much more than a girl, herself, wanted rest.

"Okay honey, I'll sing to you. Here's one. Hush little baby, don't say a word."

The little girl, just over two, laughed as her mother continued.

"Momma's gonna buy you a mockingbird."

Before she could continue, a shot rang out just beyond the window. Screaming and shouting could be heard throughout the tiny apartment. More gunshots were fired. The young mother grabbed her little child, who was no longer laughing but crying, and cradled her in her arms and ran to the bathroom.

"We'll be safe in here," she whispered to calm her child.

"If that mockingbird don't sing…"

* * *

It was the same street, but a different night. It was cold and starting to snow, so the young mother bundled the child as warmly as she could in a car seat. She pulled her ragged stocking cap over her short, blonde hair and jumped into the front seat of the little Honda. She backed out of her parking spot at the decaying building and screeched the tires as she drove frantically away from the apartment and from him.

"You'll be okay, baby. You will. Momma's gonna take care of you. Nothing's gonna hurt you anymore."

As she finished saying this, the young mother turned to her child. The child's tiny hand was resting on the padding of her car seat. She shuddered when she saw the cigarette burn again. It was no longer oozing.

She drove to the only place she could think of for the safety of her child. She'd met the lady at the food kitchen. She'd hoped to develop a friendship. Maybe she could get some counseling. Now, though, she needed more. She slammed the brakes and stopped the car in front of the store-front building. It wasn't closing time.

They were still there. She'd decided that morning, after Sara had been burned, that she had to do something. She'd seen a glimpse of a better life from the people at the shelter. She knew it was going to be tough for her, but she wanted her daughter to have a chance and to be safe. She jumped out of the car and opened the back door. Sara laughed and grabbed her hair.

"Sara, you silly girl. You have to let go now."

As she said it, she was overcome by the reality of the words she'd just uttered. She carried the car seat and had Sara walk by her, holding her hand. She knocked at the door of the shelter and then bent down to talk to Sara.

"Mommy's gonna leave you here for a while, okay baby? It'll be all right."

Sara looked at her mom.

"Okay, Mommy. Come back, okay?"

The young mother choked back tears as she knowingly lied, "I will baby. You'll see."

As she spoke, the lady came to the door. The young mom accompanied Sara in, and in an hour or so, she left. Sara never saw her again.

***

IT was a school party. Sara was in the seventh grade. It was one of those "Dad and Daughter Dances" when a girl's dad puts on a suit and comes with his daughter, stands around, dances a little and goes home. Sara stood by the food table, talking to some of the other girls. Her foster father had brought her and two other girls to the dance. He was nice enough, but everyone knew who he was and, more importantly, who he wasn't.

Sara's best friend, Emily, stood by her and they talked about boys and classes. Elaine made her way to the table. Elaine was not Sara's friend.

"Hey Sara, Em, what's going on? Is this a great party or what?"

Sara would've liked to tell Elaine to get lost. Emily, though, spoke to her.

"Yeah, it's okay."

"Well, it'd be better if our dads weren't here. How lame is that? You are so lucky Sara. I guess not having a dad can be good. You don't have a dad to embarrass you. You just have a goofy foster something or another."

Elaine might've had more to say, but Sara and Emily didn't ever hear it. Sara unloaded a right hook to Elaine's nose. She dropped. Her nose was bloodied and broken. Sara was told to leave. Her foster father called her foster mother to come and get her. It was the first time she'd been kicked out of an event. It wouldn't be the last.

***

My heart was breaking as each scene played out in my mind. It was agonizing watching what my selfishness had caused for my daughter and her mother. Sara paused in her rant and I took a deep breath.

"There's nothing I can say, Sara, except I'm sorry."

"Like that means anything now? Hey, I don't know you and don't care to know you. So you and this girl can just go away."

She put on her sun glasses and started up the hill to the Ranger.

"Sara, please. Wait. Please listen."

She stopped a few feet from the truck and turned back. A pained and puzzled expression emerged from behind the dark glasses.

"How'd you find out about me anyway?"

"George Swisher; he told me about you. He told me you'd be here."

"George? You know him? How? When did you see him last?"

"Just a few minutes ago."

I knew as I said it, I'd made a mistake. Time and events might not be the same for her as they were for me and Sun-Hi.

"You're a liar! George died this afternoon. You said you were stabbed this morning? Well, *Daddy,* why don't you just go ahead and die and leave me alone."

She slammed the door of the Ranger, revved the engine and sprayed the gravel as she left. Sun-Hi got up from the bench and walked over to me.

"What do we do now?" she asked.

Chapter Six

As she sped down the gravel drive and back onto Mill Creek Road, Sara had tears in her eyes. This time, however, they were not tears of sadness. She was angry. She wasn't really a "crier," but she'd been brought to tears twice today.

What was that all about? Hasn't this day been bad enough without some guy prancing in claiming to be my dad and wanting to help? Forget that. I don't need help. Michael's right, partly. I get in on this deal and I'm set for life. I'll quit Danny's, leave this stupid little town. Go somewhere new and start over. There's gotta be a better life somewhere. I know there is.

She accelerated down Lancaster Pike. It was still a few hours before six. She'd get some stuff from the trailer and pack it, stop by Danny's and then get out to the "meeting." From there, well, the plan was a bit fuzzy, but she knew she didn't want to stay in Delhart. She really didn't want to continue with Michael and his thugs either. *Just score this big one and don't look back.* That seemed like the best option.

***

I STOOD watching as Sara tore away in the Ranger. Sun-Hi had asked a question, but I didn't really hear it. This didn't work out at all like I thought it would. Seeing all that she'd been through, though, it was no surprise she was angry. Why wouldn't she be? She'd had a really hard life in large part because I was nowhere to be found. I was one of the biggest reasons why her life was the mess it was. What was I thinking? How could I expect her to come running to me with open arms?

"Come on, Sun-Hi. I think I know where we need to go."

"Back to see what George was going to say?"

"Yep. I don't know where else to go."

We drove back to Swisher Tires in silence. Sun-Hi didn't say anything and I continued to run through, in my mind, how the encounter with Sara had gone so badly. We pulled into the empty lot and took the same parking space as before. Sun-Hi got out and walked around to my side of the Jeep. She knocked at the window. I rolled it down.

"Aren't you coming, Greg?"

"Yeah, just a second."

I took a deep breath and composed myself. I wasn't sure if George was still in the old shop, and, if he was there, whether he would be angry at how I had fouled things up. Maybe God was mad at me, too. Either way, though, it was time to find out. I opened the door and stepped down beside Sun-Hi.

"Okay, kid. Let's go see if he's still there."

WE walked through the front door, past the reception desk and out into the garage. We didn't see George there and I didn't really expect he'd be in those places. We made it through the stacked tires and dodged the grease spots to the back of the garage. The door of the back office was cracked open a bit and a light shone through it. I figured that's where he'd be. We came up to the door and pushed it slightly. It moved a bit and we saw him sitting behind the desk in the swivel chair.

"George," I said, "You're still here."

He looked up with more of a smirk than a smile.

"I kind of thought you'd be back. Sit down. You, too, kid. How did it go?"

Sun-Hi and I sat. As I started to talk, he fumbled under the desk and pulled out a soda for Sun-Hi.

"It didn't," I stated flatly. "She didn't want to have anything to do with me, much less want my help. It was a total fail. I think she'd prefer if Sun-Hi and I left and never saw her again."

George sat back in the chair, just listening. Sun-Hi sipped the soda and watched. I was waiting, wanting George to say something. He didn't, so I spoke.

"I suppose we'll go. I failed at this big chance to do something. What happens now, I just die or what?"

George leaned forward and put his hands on the desk.

"Is that it, Greg? She doesn't come running into your arms, thanking you for showing up, so you're done? I suppose you could leave, if that's what you want to do."

"Hey, wait a minute! I didn't say I wanted to be done, but she wants nothing to do with me! I can't help her if she refuses it. She doesn't want a dad. I don't blame her, but what can I do about it?"

George was nearly across the desk now. His face smoldered with intensity.

"You need to hear what I'm about to say, so I hope you're listening."

I sat back in my chair a bit.

"Okay, yeah, go ahead."

"When you were a little boy, you were kind and considerate. You made a decision to follow Jesus and you were baptized. You loved your mom and dad. When your little sister came around, you adored her. Then an awful thing happened to Amber. When it did, something terrible happened to you, too. You began to live your life for one person; you. Your feelings about losing Amber were real and hard to work through. You didn't always have the right help either. But you never got past that. You became absorbed with making sure you were at the center of your life. Almost everything you've ever done since then has been about you in some form or another. You felt sorry for yourself, so you decided that you would dedicate *your* life to making *you* feel better. You started hanging with the neighborhood thugs because it made you feel good. You moved on to the drug trade because you were the big dog. You used girls as objects for your own pleasure and didn't even hang around long enough to know that one of them was carrying your child."

It was hard to hear this from a stranger after having envisioned it with Sara, but, in a weird way, I was relieved to get it out in the open.

"To put it bluntly, my friend, you've lived most of your life in the most selfish way possible."

I hung my head.

"Yeah, you're right. I guess I deserve what's coming to me."

At that George practically jumped the desk.

"Now you're on the right track! The truth is all of us deserve what is coming to us. But don't you remember? That's why Jesus died! He paid the price so you wouldn't have to. You knew that as a boy and you called out to him this morning. He heard your prayer and he wants you to know that no, you don't deserve heaven. You don't deserve to live. You don't deserve anything good. But because he loves you, he offers it to you, if you'll trust him. You used to, Greg. You did as a boy. Heaven only knows why you waited until the very last second of life, but you called out to him again today. You don't deserve the gift you're soon to get, but he bought it for you."

I couldn't look at George as he spoke with so much passion and love. Tears formed in my eyes, though, as I heard his words. It wasn't the first time I'd heard them.

❉ ❉ ❉

I HELD Amber's hand as we went up the stairs of the old church building. Mom and Dad were downstairs in their own class. They let me take Amber and then I went to the first grade room.

"I'll pick you up after class, "I told her as I dropped her off at the preschool room.

She didn't even look back as she ran to join her friends and teachers. I walked down to my class where Miss Lily was teaching. Miss Lily had married a few months back, but she still let us call her "Miss" Lily. She had dark brown hair and a huge smile that lit up the room. She was the prettiest girl I'd met, besides Mom. Miss Lily had all of us first graders gather around her in a circle. We sang a song; "Jesus Loves Me." After the song, she was going to tell us a story from the Bible. Before she started, though, she said she had to tell us something important.

"Remember kids, Jesus loves you, always. We get to go to heaven, not because we're good, because nobody is good all of the time. We get to go because we know him."

* * *

CHAPLAIN Kevin had just finished teaching the Bible study for the day. I'd hung around, somewhat because he'd interested me, but mostly because I didn't want to go back to the tedium of my cell.

"Hey Chap," I called out to him. "Do you think God can really forgive our sins and forget them? You know, remove them as far as the east is from the west?"

He stopped putting his books in his bag and looked me in the eye.

"Greg, I do. I don't know how he does it, and I can't always forgive as he does, but he does it. I'm sure of it."

"You think people like us here can really go to heaven? What about all the bad stuff we've done?"

"He can forgive it."

"I don't know, Chap. I've done some pretty awful things. It'll take a whole lot of good to balance out the junk I've done."

"Hold it, Greg. That's not how it works. You can't

do stuff to balance the scales. None of us can. It's all on Jesus. It's called grace in the Bible."

✳ ✳ ✳

I'D heard what George was telling me. I looked up at him, through tears.

"George, I get it. I know that's how it works. I'm pretty sure that's why I called out to him when I did."

George leaned back in the chair again and put his hands on the desk.

"I think you do get it, Greg. But there's something else."

"Yeah. I really do want to help Sara. I know I haven't been a dad to her and never will be. But she's in trouble and I'm sure I can do something."

George smiled.

"You can. Earlier you went out to her on a mission as much for you as it was for her. You wanted to be the big shot. You wanted her to see you and talk to you. You wanted her to recognize you as her father. It failed miserably. You had to get to a point where you could see that this task wasn't going to be about you or for you. She won't recognize you as her father or acknowledge that any time soon, nor should she. You won't get the warm embrace or the joy of hearing her lovingly call you 'Dad.' There are consequences for what we do on this earth. It doesn't mean there isn't forgiveness, but conse-quences remain."

I looked up at George. There weren't any more tears.

"I do understand. You're right. Of course you are. You're with the Lord. I was in this whole thing for me.

Going out to the shelter, doing that was about me, too. But George, I don't care about any of that now. I've got to do something or Sara's going to make the same stupid mistakes I did. I know in heaven every tear is wiped away, but I couldn't stand to think I could've helped her avoid this path and failed. What can I do?"

George rested his hands on the desk.

"I'm pretty sure she's dealing drugs, using too, but that's not the big thing right now. She's got a deal happening today that she thinks will set her up for life. She has to get to the old Willard place at six o'clock. I'll show you where that is."

He took out an old county map from the middle desk drawer and unfolded it.

After pointing out the route to take, he continued, "As I see it, if you can keep her from getting there, it could be enough to make a difference."

"Is that all I need to do? It doesn't sound, I don't know, very big?"

George smiled.

"Nope. You don't have to do something big. Just do your part and God will do the rest."

"Keep her from getting to the Willard place at six o'clock? That's it?"

"Yep."

"That will help her?"

"More than you can possibly know. Hey, you might need this," George said as he pointed to a tool box. "Take it. You never know how it might come in handy."

"Thanks," I replied and picked up the tool box.

Sun-Hi hugged George and then we made our way

one last time through the garage.

✳ ✳ ✳

In the parking lot of the convenience store the two men stood around the old Ford, drinking sodas and eating peanuts. The tension was growing as the clock continued toward six o'clock. The cell phone buzzed again and the younger of the two guys answered. He spoke briefly to the person on the other end. In just a minute or so, he ended the call and turned to his partner.

"Confirmation. The informant just checked in. All of the big time players are coming. It's time for us to get in place. The others will, too."

"Good," the older fellow answered as he crushed out his cigarette. "We'll get them all."

They climbed back into the old Ford and slowly backed away from the convenience store. They drove down Main Street, past the early evening traffic and onto the highway. It wouldn't be long now.

✳ ✳ ✳

Sara parked the truck in front of her trailer. For a moment she just sat, her mind was racing, replaying all that had happened since she'd left this morning. She still had the stash Michael had given her. It was safely in the bag just under the passenger seat. The money bag with the rest that Manny had delivered was also there. She carried her gun under that seat, too. In a different bag she had over seven thousand dollars in hundred dollar bills. That, too, was under the passenger seat, with the coke and the gun. She checked her watch. It was already close to five o'clock. Time was moving. For a moment she thought of George and Frances, their family. It made her sad to think that she'd never see him or any of them again. A thought pushed aside that sadness.

It is what it is.

She got out of the truck, grabbed her purse and found the trailer keys. She stepped up onto the porch and unlocked the door.

This will be the last time I do this.

The trailer door creaked as Sara opened it. She paused in the narrow living room, surveying all of her earthly possessions. It wasn't much. She walked the short hallway back to her bedroom. She slid open the hollow wood closet door, grabbed a handful of the clothes hanging there and threw them onto the bed. She found a beat-up suitcase and threw in the few things she thought were acceptable and vital. She decided she'd just leave the rest here. It wasn't really the way to do things, but at this point, what difference did it make? She was leaving town anyway. She'd start over somewhere else. She lugged the battered suitcase out of the trailer and threw it from the porch to the grass. She took one final glance around the trailer, and, feeling no nostalgia, slammed the door shut. She didn't even bother locking it. She picked up the suitcase, threw it in the back of the Ranger, and climbed in. As she turned the ignition, her mind was fixated on getting the deal done and getting out.

Chapter Seven

The Willard family had been around Delhart for as long as anyone could remember. At one time, the Willard farm was a showcase home; a sprawling, three-story farmhouse set back a quarter mile from the road. It was a beautiful brick structure, with black shutters and white pillars holding the roof over the front porch. Wicker chairs usually sat on the front porch, and on many nights Mr. and Mrs. Willard could be found sitting there, sipping tea and watching the evening fade into night. The grass was always neatly cut, and the gravel roads that connected the house, the horse barn, and tool shed were well-kept and maintained. A small pond was located to the right of the driveway and it was always stocked with small fish. Guthrie Willard was a successful farmer and well-respected throughout the area. His grandpa was one of the first to use the canals for which Delhart, at one time, was famous. He and his father got even richer when the trucking industry exploded onto the scene. He sold his soybean crop all across the northern part of the state and beyond. From Guthrie's time on, the Willard family never lacked. They always had plenty of money and anything else that they may have wanted. Guthrie worked hard, twelve or fourteen hours a day, to make sure that happened. Unfortunately, while his heirs got his money, they did not inherit his work ethic. Guthrie's kids got used to having money and not having to work hard for it and that trait was passed on and magnified. Now, four generations later, the old house was occupied by the remaining Willards; Colby and his sister, Arlene.

The brick farmhouse still sat back from the road, but the porch was sagging; the paint on the pillars had chipped and faded. A few of the black shutters were missing while others hung crookedly, missing some bolt or screw. Weeds had grown up around the old tool shed, almost making it disappear. The barn was still standing, housing farm equipment that hadn't been started in over twenty years. Old gas cans still littered the dirty floor. The water in the pond was a sickly green and no one was quite sure what might be found at the bottom of it. This was the current condition of the Willard place. Arlene and Colby lived here. It was their family inheritance. They had each been married a couple of times and had several "live-in" significant others, but no matter what, they all stayed at the Willard place. They made some money dabbling in part-time jobs, but never had much to show for it. What little they had was burned up in drugs. A bit of great-grandpa's money remained, but not much. The Willard place once made residents of Delhart proud. Now it was an eyesore and a disgrace.

"Pull in at the next gravel road," the younger man told the older who was driving the old Ford. "That's where we're supposed to wait."

They passed the driveway to the old farmhouse. A rusting pick-up truck and a newer foreign car were the only ones in the drive.

"Got it," the driver replied as he pulled the cigarette from his mouth. "Looks like both Willards are in."

"Yep," the younger one replied. "It's quiet now, but not for long."

They came to the next gravel turn off, a few hundred feet from the drive. The older man slowly turned the Ford into the gravel and gently backed it around so that it sat facing the street.

"We'll wait here until it's time."

The younger man nodded.

"Hard to believe this is really going down."

✳✳✳

I LEFT Swisher's tire store knowing that I wouldn't come back again. Sun-Hi and I got into the Jeep and backed slowly out of the empty parking lot. As I pulled onto Arcadia, I stopped. There was no traffic, nor did I expect there to be any.

"What are we doing, Greg?" Sun-Hi asked.

"I need to think a minute," I answered, "maybe even pray."

She nodded and looked out of the window at the vast nothingness that was Delhart. A few cows ate grass in a nearby field. I knew what I had to do. I had a precious few minutes to try to stop Sara from getting to that meeting. George had told me where that was, so I was fairly sure of the route she'd take. I knew what I was supposed to do, but how? How do you stop someone from getting to where they want to go? My thoughts were interrupted by Sun-Hi tapping me on the shoulder.

"Greg, I don't mean to interrupt, but I think we ought to be going."

"Sun-Hi, you aren't interrupting me... Wait, that's it, Sun-Hi! You're brilliant!"

I leaned over and kissed her on the forehead.

"We won't try to stop her. We'll just interrupt her trip."

I slammed the Jeep into drive and squealed the tires as we sped down Arcadia and onto Main Street. In no time at all we were on Lancaster Pike headed out toward the Willard place. At a fork in the road, I smashed the brakes and we came to a jerking stop, frightening Sun-Hi.

"Sorry, kid," I told her as I jumped out of the Jeep and ran behind it.

I quickly located the tool box George had given me and found the wire cutters. I jumped over the ditch that lined Lancaster Pike and soon found myself next to the barbed wire fence. The cows had wandered over to check out the crazy guy with the wire cutters. In a matter of minutes I had cut three strands of barbed wire. I ran to the cows inside and began pushing and yelling at them to move out of the fence and into the road. Sun-Hi jumped across the ditch to help. It took several minutes, but finally we managed to get six cows to stand in and around Lancaster Pike. I was pretty sure they were not in any danger. They would be there for one car, a truck rather, a green Ford Ranger.

✱✱✱

As Sara drove down Main toward Lancaster Pike, she felt her heart pounding in her chest. She went through the checklist one more time; *money, stash, suitcase, gun.* One more deal and it was over. She'd have money and a chance for a new life. Her hands shook as she gripped the steering wheel. She couldn't help it. This was the biggest deal she'd ever seen. She pulled her phone out of her purse and called Michael.

"Hey, just checking in," she told him.

"Yeah, good. Manny and I are nearly there. Don't be late or you'll get cut out. Big Man from across the border is coming. Wants to make the transaction himself."

Sara listened and muttered an affirmation as Michael continued.

"Okay, girl. Gotta go. See you in a while. Don't be late. Once the deal's going down, no one gets in."

"Got it."

Sara put the phone back in her purse as she pulled onto Lancaster Pike. There was no traffic, which was a bit surprising. She glanced at the time displayed on her phone; 5:42. She should make it easily. She took a deep breath and sped up. As she crested the first hill, she slammed on the brakes. Six cows were standing in the middle of the highway. No one was around. She skidded to a stop and blared the horn.

"Get out of the way!"

She continued to honk and drive up closer to the cows. They wouldn't budge. She looked and saw the barbed wire down on a section of fence by the road.

"Unbelievable," she said to no one in particular.

"How does this happen?"

She got out of the Ranger and began shooing cattle.

***

Sun-Hi and I sped away from the cows. I knew that would take up some of Sara's time, but I wanted to "interrupt" once more. We drove down Lancaster Pike as George had shown me. At last we came to the country road that led to our destination. After turning there, I parked the Jeep and we waited. A minute or two passed and a Chevy truck turned quickly off Lancaster onto the county road, spraying gravel everywhere. I saw two men in the truck. Right behind them a silver Cadillac made a wide turn from the highway onto the narrow county road.

"That's them," I told Sun-Hi as we watched them pass. I doubted if they saw us at all.

"Sun-Hi, we have to create a road block here. Something she'll have to stop to get through. Look around and try to find something we can use."

"Greg, look," Sun-Hi exclaimed as she pointed to a dead and decaying tree lying off the side of the road.

"Yeah, that might work."

We ran to what was left of the tree. I grabbed it in a bear-hug and Sun-Hi tried pushing from the other side.

"It won't budge," she cried.

"You're right," I told her, "we'll have to cut it. Quick, get the saw from the tool box."

Sun-Hi ran to the Jeep and brought me the saw. I began trying to cut through the rot and decay in an effort to bring the tree down.

"Hurry Greg," Sun-Hi implored, "she could be com-

74

ing down the road any minute."

I ran that saw through the wood as fast as I could. As I did I kept watch down Lancaster, hoping, praying that I wouldn't see a green Ford Ranger. At last, there was a cracking at the center of the dead tree. It was breaking apart.

"Come on, Sun-Hi. Let's get this thing out into the road."

Sun-Hi and I pulled the biggest part of the tree into the middle of the gravel road, just down from the turn off of Lancaster Pike. I hustled back to grab a second and third section and threw them into the road as well. She'd have to at least stop the truck and get out to move them. That might be just enough time. We jumped back into the Jeep.

"Come on," I called to Sun-Hi, "we've got one more thing to do. I don't know for sure if this will work, but I've got to believe it will."

Sun-Hi looked at me, puzzled.

"I'm sure the law enforcement folks have been following and keeping up with Sara. I'm pretty sure they know how many are supposed to come to this gathering. They've got to see what they think is Sara pulling in there. Once the raid starts and arrests are made, they won't worry about her not being there. They may wait, though, if they expect her to come. We have to make them think we're her."

"Do you think they'll be able to see us? Most people can't."

"I don't know for sure, but I trust the Lord will make it happen."

I continued to accelerate down the gravel road. We were less than a mile away from the house. I gunned it. The Jeep bounced along the gravel road. Sun-Hi had to hold on. As we came upon the house, I craned my neck to see what was in the drive. Two trucks, one of them rusted, a small foreign car and a big Cadillac were already there. While I was looking, I missed the entrance to the driveway.

"Hey Greg," Sun-Hi called out. "You were supposed to turn there."

"Shoot! You're right Sun-Hi. I'll turn around at the next drive."

I saw the gravel drive just ahead and quickly spun the Jeep around. I barely touched the brakes. As we made the quick turn, I noticed a car parked in the gravel drive. I figured they saw us, too.

✻ ✻ ✻

THE driver of the old Ford reached for another cigarette.

"Hey," his partner bantered, "isn't that your third one in an hour?"

"Yeah, so what? I get bored just waiting here."

At that moment the younger one's cell phone buzzed.

"Okay. Got it. Right. Report when all are in place. Yep."

"What was that all about?"

"Things are starting to move. Our spotter says the truck and the Cadillac are on their way. We should see them shortly. Once the Ford Ranger girl arrives, it's a go. We're to let them know."

The older one took a puff of the cigarette and picked up the binoculars. He peered through the trees to the drive of the Willard place.

"You're right. I see the truck and caddy just pulling in. Once the gal gets there, we give the signal."

The older of the two took another draw on the cigarette and flicked the ashes out the window of the Ford. A slight breeze was blowing and the ash was still smoldering a bit. Some of it blew back into the car.

"Hey! Watch it!" his partner shouted as he jumped back and tried to flick away the embers. "You'll set this old clunker on fire if you're not careful."

As they brushed away the cigarette ash, a Jeep flew down the gravel road and did a quick stop, sending gravel flying. In a matter of seconds it had turned around and was moving back toward the Willard place. The two glanced up quickly.

"Hey, did you see that?"

"Was that her? I saw two in there."

"She must've dumped the Ranger for a Jeep. Smart gal. I did see one female and one male. I'm pretty sure it's them. Besides, who else would be going to the Willard place?"

"Do we signal them?"

"Yep, it's time."

***

Sara finally got the cows off Lancaster Pike. The time flashed on her phone; 5:53. She'd have to really hurry now. She jumped in and cranked the ignition. She gunned the Ranger down the highway at nearly a hundred miles an hour. In just a couple of minutes she was at the country road that led to the Willard place. Without checking who might be behind her, she turned the Ranger onto the country road and slammed the brakes once again. A dead tree was lying in the middle of the road. It was too big to drive over. She turned off the truck, threw open the door and swore.

***

I DROVE up the driveway of the Willard place, turned onto the weed-infested gravel drive that led to the barn and parked the Jeep there. I was pretty sure that Sun-Hi and I were out of sight in more ways than one. I had no sooner turned off the engine when we heard it. There must've been ten or twelve police cars; a couple of SWAT team vans and nearly a legion of armed officers and drug enforcement officials descending on the Willard place. Three or four passed right by the Jeep without even noticing that we were there. I was now confident that the Lord had brought us back out of the "real" world into the one we'd been in all day. There was shouting and several gun shots. In a matter of minutes, several people, men and women, were being led out of the house. Apparently more were there than just the Willards. As we watched the spectacle in silence, Sun-Hi tapped my shoulder.

"Look," she said. "There she is."

I turned and saw the green Ford Ranger. She passed the Willard place and hurried down the gravel road. I smiled.

"We did it, Sun-Hi."

* * *

It took her about five minutes to drag the dead tree out of the road, but Sara was determined. Once she had a narrow path around it, she jumped back into the truck and fired up the engine. The time on her phone flashed a minute after six, but she still thought she might make it. She accelerated over the first hill and crushed the brakes for a third time. There were police, SWAT teams and DEA everywhere! Her heart nearly stopped beating. No one was looking for her, so she sped by the Willard place. When she had driven about five or six miles out into the country, she pulled over and jumped out of the truck. She grabbed several things from the truck and ran into the woods as far as she could until she came to a cliff. She took the stash, the money and the gun and threw them over the side. They landed somewhere in the brush and debris that collected below. It would be a long time before anyone would find them. Sara collapsed on the dirt and grass near the edge of the cliff and threw up. After lying there for a few minutes, she walked back to the truck. She reached for her purse and took out her phone. She pushed a number and held the phone to her ear.

"Hey Grant, it's me, Sara. Can I come over and see you and Frances? Yeah, I heard. I know. I'm really sorry too. Yeah, I'll be right over. Thanks."

Chapter Eight

Sun-Hi and I drove through the confusion and chaos at the Willard place and back into downtown Delhart. It was abandoned as I expected it to be. I turned off of Main and back onto the highway leading out of town. The sun seemed to be setting. It was evening now, though time hadn't really been a factor so far.

"Greg," Sun-Hi said as we passed by the empty convenience store, "will you stop there for a minute please?"

I eased the Jeep into the abandoned store lot.

"What's up, Sun-Hi? Are you all right? You aren't sick, are you?"

"No. I'll be right back."

She jumped out of the Jeep and ran inside. I expected her to come back with a soda or some snack, but she didn't. She clutched a newspaper in her hand.

"Why do you want that?" I asked her as she climbed back in.

"I need to check something," she replied.

We pulled out of the lot, got back on the highway and headed out of Delhart.

"Sun-Hi, I don't know about you, but I'm feeling really good right now."

She nodded and kept looking at the paper.

"I think it's probably one of the only things I've done in my life that wasn't for me or that no one really knew about. How do you think she'll do? What do you think will happen to her?"

Sun-Hi turned to me and said, "I think you'll get to find out, Greg."

I continued to drive, but was puzzled by her answer.

"What do you mean? How will I get to know?"

"You'll see," was her reply.

I stopped the Jeep at the stop sign that led back onto the highway. At this point I wasn't sure what to do.

"Okay, kid, what's next? Is it back to Lucasville for the finale?"

Sun-Hi shook her head and said, "Greg, have you ever been to Hamilton County? I think it's near Cincinnati."

I was startled by her question.

"Why do you ask?"

"I just read through this article in the paper and the name of a person and a place kind of stuck out to me."

"Who? What article are you reading?"

"Her name is Yolanda Dennison. She lives in Hamilton County at 12 Jefferson Street. At least, that's what this article says. I think that's where we're supposed to go."

She ignored my other question. I sighed.

"You mean helping Sara wasn't enough? There's more that I'm supposed to do?"

Sun-Hi looked up at me. Her silence spoke more than words ever might.

"Okay. I'm sorry, kid. I've got more mistakes than

almost anyone I know. I'll do it. We'll go to Hamilton County. What's the address?"

I punched the address into the GPS as Sun-Hi and I had done before, then turned left and headed south. As had been the case earlier, there were no other cars on the highway. We were alone.

"Sun-Hi, I never heard of Yolanda Dennison. Do you know if she's going to tell us what to do or is she the one we're supposed to help?"

"I don't know, Greg."

The drive that should've taken nearly two hours went by very quickly. It was clear to me that time was not relevant for us. It wasn't long before we heard the GPS telling us to take the next exit and turn left.

***

THE houses in the Terrace Gardens subdivision were laid out neatly in rows. Six houses on each side of a street named after a former president. The whole neighborhood was circled by Garden Drive which connected to Westwood Avenue which led to the highway. At one time it had been a growing, middle-class subdivision with new families moving in and wonderful neighborhood schools. In the late seventies, drugs and crime became more prevalent in Hamilton County, but Terrace Gardens, though not quite what it once was, still maintained a level of quality living. It was still a middle-class neighborhood with good schools. The folks that lived there were proud of how they kept what many had lost.

✳✳✳

Sᴜɴ-Hɪ and I turned off the highway onto Westwood. In a few minutes we stopped at the light leading to Garden Drive. I turned the Jeep onto Garden Drive and the GPS brought us to Jefferson Street. The house we were looking for was the third one on the right. We passed the first couple of ranch style homes; the second one had a garage and a basketball goal in the driveway. I parked the Jeep in front of the house with the number "12" by the door and looked around.

"There isn't anyone here, Sun-Hi."

She nodded and reached for the newspaper again.

"Do we just go up and knock?"

Sun-Hi shrugged.

We both got out of the Jeep and walked slowly to the front porch of the abandoned house; 12 Jefferson Street. I opened the screen door and looked at Sun-Hi. I suppose I was hoping to gain some courage from my young traveling companion. She just looked back at me, confused as I was. This situation was strange. Earlier, we'd gone back to my hometown and, in what seemed like a lifetime ago, we saw my mom. She told us about George Swisher. He was easy to find. This was different, though. No one had said to come here. Sun-Hi just felt like it was right from reading an article which I had yet to even read!

"Here goes."

I started to knock. I moved my hand but at that very instant the door opened.

An older lady wearing a patterned dress loosely around her thin frame pulled open the door. She had wavy, gray hair and wire-rimmed glasses. A hearing aid was visible in her left ear. I was fairly sure of who she was.

"Uh, excuse me. Are you Yolanda Dennison?"

"Good evening," the woman called out, practically ignoring my question. "I've been expecting you. If you don't mind, let's sit out here on the porch. I loved sitting out here come an evening. It's real pretty."

Yolanda took the patio chair that she'd sat in for years. Sun-Hi took the one opposite Yolanda. I sat in her porch swing. She leaned back, closed her eyes and breathed in deeply.

"Uh, I think I'd better introduce us. I'm Greg and this is Sun-Hi."

"I know who you are," she croaked. "I also know why you're here."

"Mrs. Dennison," I began.

"Call me Yo," she interrupted. "I always went by Yo."

"All right, Yo," I continued, "My friend and I are here because we think we've been sent here. We don't exactly know why, but we're sure that you can tell us something that will help us on our, uh, journey."

Yolanda smiled.

"I see," she said. "So just what do you want to know from me?"

I looked to Sun-Hi and then around the empty neighborhood. It all seemed so weird.

"I don't know. Sun-Hi thinks we're supposed to come here, but I'm beginning to think it's a mistake."

Yolanda leaned forward in her chair.

"A mistake? You've made a lot of those, haven't you, Greg? Suppose you tell me why you spent nearly thirty years in prison."

She knew my name and my history, but at this point, everyone we met seemed to know that stuff.

"I killed a guy. He wasn't that good of a guy, but I guess he didn't deserve to die. He and I worked the drug trade together. He stole from me and I killed him."

She looked over her glasses at me.

"Let me see that article you read, Sun-Hi," Yolanda said.

Sun-Hi gave it to her and she adjusted her glasses to read it. As she read it she frowned, took a tissue from her purse and dabbed her eyes.

"So, what's it about?" I asked.

"The headline is 'Teen Killed in Botched Drug Deal.'"

"So, what's that got to do with me?"

I was getting a bit agitated. Yolanda folded the paper and gave it back to Sun-Hi.

"Let me tell you my story. It won't take long, I promise."

I pushed back in the swing and it rocked gently.

"Sure," I answered, "go ahead."

"The boy in the article, he was a good boy. His family lived right over there."

She pointed to the house next door.

"He lived with his momma and daddy. Tré was his name. He was an only child and they loved him more than words could say. His momma spoiled him a bit, but not bad. His daddy worked hard to provide for all of them. He was a big, strong fella. He worked construction and was good at it. There wasn't anything he couldn't build. He did for all of us in the neighborhood, too. He was doing all right for a while, but then things got tough. He lost his job. I thought sure they'd have to move; so many did. But somehow, he found work. In fact, he was making more money than ever. For a year or so, things were great. You couldn't ask for better neighbors. And Tré? That boy was smart. He made straight A's in school and could play little league like you wouldn't believe. He was such a helpful boy. He came over here and swept my porch, weeded my flower beds or whatever chores needed doing. Never took any money. Those were good times; real good. Good times, though, didn't last. Tré's daddy, Walter, started being away from home more. I thought maybe he'd taken an out of town job, but that wasn't it. He showed up from time to time, but he'd changed. He wasn't the fun-loving, doting daddy anymore. He'd gotten, I don't know, harder, I guess. He stopped playing ball with Tré. He seemed to be consumed with whatever job he had. They had money all right, but I could tell JoAnne, Tré's momma, wasn't happy. Things kept getting worse, until it all broke apart. On a rainy morning a whole group of police cars came pulling in here. One of them even parked in my driveway. They all went over to JoAnne's. I didn't know why, but found out later. The whole neighborhood found out. Walter McKinnick had been killed in a drug deal. He left his wife, JoAnne and his son, Walter McKinnick III, Tré. It all made sense then. I understood what had happened to him and how they were able to still have money. Walter had been working with some crooks and thugs. I guess he crossed the wrong one and ended up dead.

At that point, the whole neighborhood tried to pitch in and help JoAnne. I knew she and the boy had to be devastated. I always thought she knew what Walter had been doing, but didn't want to face it. Now, though, she had no choice. They had a little insurance policy, which he'd had from a previous job that allowed her and Tré to stay in the house. After a long time, I think JoAnne began to heal. She continued to go to church. She got a job with the school district. She and Tré were making it; well, almost. Tré didn't handle his daddy's death very well. He was angry and didn't understand. He missed his daddy and, in some ways, admired him, even though he got shot in a drug deal. It was almost as if he wanted to follow his daddy's footsteps. He found some fellas to hang with, a rotten group. I know JoAnne hated that. She tried all she could to steer him away from that crowd, but she was a single momma and couldn't be everywhere. Tré sort of grew up without any good role models. He was nine years old when his daddy died. By the time he was twelve, he'd been arrested twice for shoplifting. It was that horrible crowd he chose to hang with. He was smart and the street gangs knew it. They used him. He didn't care. Since his daddy was gone, he just did whatever he wanted or whatever the gang told him to do. It was almost as if he stopped valuing life itself. He wanted to be like his daddy. I know JoAnne was beside herself with worry. All of us in the neighborhood knew we were watching a disaster just waiting to happen. It was like watching two trains on the same track heading toward each other. You can see it coming, but what can you do? Lots of folks tried talking to that boy, but by the time he was fifteen, he wasn't a boy anymore. He'd grown big like his daddy had been. Now, he wasn't just running with the "bad kids," he was in deep with some real trouble. He was strong, smart and had a mean streak. He thought he was invincible. I suppose he thought that right up until they shot him dead just across the highway. It was awful. JoAnne moved away. She lived by herself in a high-rise building in Columbus. I didn't hear much about her after that."

Yolanda sighed and took a deep breath.

"If his daddy had been around and hadn't got involved in all that drug mess, I'm sure things would've been different. So, Greg, does my story involve you?"

I looked down at the porch.

"I'm the one who killed Tré's daddy. I killed Walter McKinnick."

∗ ∗ ∗

IT was a stormy night in Cincinnati. The bright lights of downtown were reflected in the rain and created a beautiful picture of the Queen City. Beauty, however, was deceptive and fleeting. The rain poured down in the darkened alley where I was waiting. There were no bright lights here. This place would never make a lovely picture. I was in the alley beside what used to be a market. It was up the hill, not far from the downtown. There were several buildings here that, at one time, were part of a booming economic center. For the last several years, though, they'd become part of urban blight. These old buildings saw a different kind of "business." Prostitutes, pimps, drug pushers, users and an assortment of petty thieves and drunks hung out here. I hated this kind of place. I was sure it was beneath me, and I didn't like associating with this crowd, but I had to meet a guy.

His name was Walter McKinnick, Jr. He went by "Junior" in my circles. I'm guessing his daddy was big into the "game," too. I never knew for sure and, frankly, never cared. I met Junior when he'd come along with a client of mine. I delivered a nice load to a fellow in Hamilton County. Junior had come along as the guy's muscle. He wasn't needed. I'd been in a few scrapes and knew how to take care of myself, but I valued my brains too much to have them scrambled in some deal gone wrong. Junior and I talked while his present employer attended to his own affairs. I liked Junior and could see right away that he had more going for him than just being a muscle guy. He had "street smarts." He also had an insatiable desire to make money. It was inevitable that we'd get together. A few months was all it took for us to gain control over the largest drug trade in the state. We networked with gang leaders and others to get the stuff and supplied some of the most influential citizens of the Buckeye state. Junior and I were bringing in more money than either of us could've imagined. Life was good, probably too good. For whatever reason, Junior got greedy. He began taking more than his share. He did it in a smart way; just a little at a time, but I'm no dummy. I could tell in a matter of weeks what was happening. Junior McKinnick had crossed the line. He needed to be reined in.

That's why I was in the alley on a dark, rainy night in downtown Cincinnati. Junior McKinnick would come by and collect from the lowlifes who sold and used junk on the streets. When he did, I'd put a bullet in him. He turned the corner after collecting cash from some doped-up teens and was startled to see me crouching there. He seemed genuinely surprised to see me and kept that surprised look on his face as the bullet hit him and he fell to the ground. He was still breathing when I took the money from him, but barely. I drove away and left the body there, expecting him to die. I guess those druggies weren't as stoned as I was thinking they were, because they described me to the police. I was arrested two days later.

***

I WRAPPED up my story and looked to Sun-Hi. She stared at me, almost without blinking. I looked to Yolanda who had her head back and her eyes closed. The silence was heavy.

"So, what do I do? Am I supposed to somehow make amends with Walter?"

"Is that what you think?" Yolanda replied.

"Well, I can see that my actions had some pretty harsh consequences for his family. I don't know. He made choices, too. Maybe I can do something?"

"You can."

"What?" I asked. "What do I need to do?"

"Confront the boy. You need to speak to Tré. Many have prayed for him. He needs to have an encounter with someone that knows where he's at and where he's headed. Frankly, you need to do whatever is necessary to bring that boy back from the path he's on."

"Can it be done? Isn't it too late? The article says he's already dead."

"It's never too late. God can change things. I would've thought you would know that by now."

"Yeah, you're right," I replied, accepting the inevitable that I would encounter the boy as I had Sara.

"When and where?" I asked Yolanda.

"He'll come by here tonight, before eight. He'll go over across the highway for the drug deal at ten. That's when he's shot. I guess you have to handle it as you're led to."

I nodded.

"Can I leave Sun-Hi here with you? I don't want her to be around for this."

"That's fine. We'll be safe here."

"He'll show up at his house around eight?"

"Yep, that's right."

"That's in less than an hour."

Chapter Nine

I watched as Sun-Hi and Yolanda went into her house. I was sure Sun-Hi would be safe. I wasn't as certain about me. I went to the Jeep to stash the keys. I wandered over to the McKinnick house. The front door was locked. I was certain that JoAnne was at work. Tré wasn't home yet; I wasn't expecting him for at least another twenty minutes. I sat on the concrete step of the porch and watched the setting sun. I'd been in prison for three decades, but I wasn't exactly a "tough" guy. I knew Tré was only fifteen, but I had a hunch he was more man than boy. I remembered how big Junior was and figured, in a matter of minutes, I'd meet a younger version. I wouldn't be able to just intimidate this kid. I also knew that I wouldn't be able to out-muscle him. I'd had a few fights in prison. Most that have done time have. I won a few; lost some, too. I'd had a broken nose and lost a couple of teeth. In the fights I managed to win, I was able to outsmart the other guy. It wasn't about brute force. It was knowing how and where to hurt your opponent. The key was to make him unable to continue fighting. Nothing else mattered. As I sat and watched the sky turn orange, I hoped I wouldn't have to fight at all. Maybe I could just talk to Tré. The thought then hit me. *He may not come alone!* That thought terrified me. I quickly looked around the yard and porch for something I could use as a weapon. There wasn't much around; only a flower garden. I didn't have much time to look, though, because, in the distance, I heard a loud muffler. Seconds later I saw a beat-up Chevy turning onto Jefferson and coming toward me. Tré was alone. I breathed a sigh of relief. He pulled into the drive and threw open the door.

"Hey, old man, why are you here? Mama's not here if you're looking for her."

I stood. Though he was only fifteen, I could see he was no child. He stood nearly six feet tall and was thick, had to weigh at least 200 pounds, all muscle. He wore a loose-fitting sweatshirt, baggy jeans and a Reds cap.

I gulped and spoke, "No. I didn't come for your mother, Tré. I came to see you."

"I don't know you old man. How do you know about me and Mama? You aren't a police officer, are you?"

I smirked.

"No, nothing like that."

"Whatever then, man. I don't have time for discussion. You'll have to hit the road. Quince will be here any minute."

He started to move toward me, expecting me to get out of the way. I stood my ground.

"Just a minute, Tré, give me a second or two to talk to you. That's all I need."

He put his hand on my chest and pushed, just a bit, to

let me know he wasn't kidding around.

"I already told you, I have places to go. Hit the road."

He pushed me again, harder this time. At that moment, I knew what I had to do. I said a quick prayer and then put both hands on his massive chest and pushed back as hard as I could. He was surprised and stumbled a bit as he fell back. He quickly recovered and I could tell he was going to retaliate. I got both hands up, but not before his big right fist crashed into the left side of my jaw. I could taste the blood in my mouth, along with another broken tooth. It didn't hurt as much as it should've, though. That was odd. He must've thought he'd ended it with one punch because he put his hands down. I got up from the ground into a crouching position. As soon as he lowered his hands, I launched myself, like a linebacker at a running back. I hit him square in the chest, surprising him for the second time. His cap went flying. I was on top of him and took that chance to land as many blows to his head and shoulders as I could. I must've hit him a dozen times or more. His nose was bleeding. He wasn't through fighting, though. After absorbing all of my punches, he freed both arms and pushed me off. I landed a few feet away from him and had just collected myself when he grabbed me by my shirt and landed another right to my face. It stung, but a haymaker like that should've knocked me out. It didn't. He hit me again, this time in the stomach. It knocked the wind out of me, but I was still standing. His inability to finish me made him get even more angry and careless. He swung hard, but wildly, with his left hand. I ducked. He swung and missed again with his right. I took that opportunity to kick him, hard, in the stomach. He doubled over. I again drove my shoulder into him, knocking him to the ground. As we fell toward the porch, I noticed some rocks in the garden. I grabbed a larger one and while sitting on his chest, I raised it high above his head. Tré looked at me. He had a surprised look on his face as if he was stunned an old man might actually take his life. It was a look that I was sure I'd seen before on his daddy's face, just before I shot him. I knew I could use that rock to bash his skull. He would be seriously injured, maybe even die. He knew it, too. I lowered my arm. I wasn't going to crush his head. I'd already killed one too many guys named Walter McKinnick. He seemed shocked by the whole encounter.

At that moment, I heard a car door slam. I immediately jumped up, still clutching the rock. Tré continue to lie on the ground.

Quince had started to run toward us, but when I turned and faced him with the rock, he backed off.

"Hey, old dude," he called out, "I don't want no trouble with you. I just came here for my boy, Tré."

"He's not going," I told him in the most intimidating voice I could muster.

"I don't know man," Quince countered, "T Max ain't gonna like that."

"You can tell T Max to…"

My words were cut off as Tré spoke. He was on his feet now, but holding his stomach.

"Hey man, go on ahead. I'll catch up with T Max later."

"You sure?"

"Yeah man. Tell him I wouldn't go with you. That way he won't blame you."

"All right," Quince answered as he got back in his car. "I'll tell him some old dude was giving you trouble."

I raised the rock again, but Quince had already started the car and was backing out onto Jefferson. As he pulled away, I dropped the rock and turned back to Tré.

"Hey," I told him, "Thanks. I know you could've gone with him. With both of you here, I couldn't have stopped you."

Tré sat down on the porch. He was rubbing his head and wincing.

"Old man, you could've killed me, but you didn't. Nobody has ever hung with me in a fight like that. I'm not sure my daddy could've done that. I had to know what it was you wanted to talk about so bad that you would fight me."

"Do you mind if I sit?" I asked him as I sat on the porch next to him.

"You are one tough guy, Tré, just like your dad was."

"Wait. You knew my dad?"

I looked at him. For the first time since he'd arrived home, he had the look of a kid rather than a fighting man.

"Yeah, I did, a little."

"Then you know he died. He got shot in some drug deal. I hated him for that. For a long time, I hated him."

I started to reply, but he continued.

"After a while, though, it came to me. He was just doing what he had to do to get us by. That's what you do. That's what I do. Mama, she doesn't get it, but I do."

"Is that how it is, Tré? You do what you have to do,

to get by? Can I ask you a few questions?"

"I guess. I still have some time."

"I knew your dad, but, like I said, not real well. Tell me what you remember."

"I told you he died."

"Not that. I know you said that. Tell me about what it was like growing up here."

He made a face, as if he hadn't thought about these memories in quite a while.

"All right, I can tell you a little."

He started and I began to see it in my mind.

***

It was a warm, summer day. The sun was high in the sky and there wasn't a cloud in sight. The little boy played in the sandbox in the backyard. His mom brought out paper plates, cups and containers of lettuce, tomatoes and onions. Ketchup and mustard bottles were already on the picnic table.

"Hey JoAnne," the man at the grill called out, "what time are they coming?"

"They should be here in less than an hour," she replied.

The boy, no more than four years old, overheard as he dug roads in the sand for his cars and trucks.

"Who's coming?"

"The Carters from across the street will be here. Mr. and Mrs. Mueller, the new couple that moved in last week said they'd come," his mother answered.

"Is Yo coming?" the boy yelled from the sandbox.

His mom smiled.

"Of course, she'll be here."

✳✳✳

IT was the same backyard, but it was evening. The boy was bigger, older. He stood in the grass, fifteen yards or so away from his dad, wearing a Reds cap. He slapped his mitt.

"Come on, Dad. Fire it in here!"

"All right, Tré, here it comes."

Tré wasn't much older than seven, but he was a big boy. His dad didn't go easy on him. He fired a pretty hard fastball. It smacked loudly in Tré's glove.

"Yeoow! That was some fastball!"

"Nice catch, Tré. Are you all right?"

"Yeah Dad, now get ready for my fastball."

He wound up and fired his best pitch. The ball popped in his dad's glove.

"Strike! Good pitch, Tré."

The game continued for at least half an hour. Finally, JoAnne called them in to eat dinner.

"You sure are strong, Dad," Tré told him as they climbed the patio stairs.

"You are too, Son."

✳✳✳

TRÉ continued to talk and the scenes he described became real in my mind. The boy was in his bedroom. He was supposed to be reading and getting ready for bed, but what he was doing was listening. His mom and dad were in the living room. If he listened closely, he could hear them.

"Walt, we can make it again. I don't mind moving. So what if it's not as good a house or neighborhood, if we're together, it'll be all right."

"No, JoAnne. We just got out of that lousy ghetto. I'm not having you and Tré back in it again. I'll do what I have to do. I'll make it work. You've gotta trust me, babe."

"I don't want you working with Robert Johns. You and I both know he's crooked. Who knows what he'll get you involved in."

"But the money is good, JoAnne. It won't be for long, just until the construction business comes back. I promise."

"Money's not the most important thing."

"Think about Tré, JoAnne. He can stay here in this house, in this neighborhood. He'll stay in the same great school. I want him to have every chance. He's smart. You know that. Let's do it for Tré."

✳✳✳

Tré stopped. I could tell he was moved recalling these stories.

"You had some good times here, huh? You miss your dad."

He looked away. I was pretty sure he didn't want me to see the tears that were forming in his eyes.

"I'm no expert on dads, but how you describe him, it seems like you and he were close."

"I guess," he replied. "But I'm done with these stories."

He glanced at his watch.

"I don't have much time if I'm going to meet T Max and Quince. Is that all you came here for; stories about my dad and growing up here?"

"No, it isn't. I guess I'd better get right to it. I've been listening to your stories and it's pretty clear to me that you had a great family. I understand your dad made some bad choices. I get why he did it, but that doesn't make it right. I know his dying left you and your mom in a tough spot."

I stood and started pacing as I continued to talk.

"Tré, your mom has been able to get through all that junk. She didn't get 'over' it as if it never touched her, but she got through it. But you didn't. You got stuck feeling sorry for yourself and doing the same stupid stuff your dad did. I don't know exactly why he took that path, but I'm pretty sure he wouldn't choose it for you. I think in some twisted, foolish way he thought he was helping you and your mom. He was wrong, tragically wrong. You're a smart guy. You can understand that. Why are you walking that same dead-end path he did? You got talent. Your dad knew that. Your mom can see it. This whole neighborhood knows you do. Tré, this is important, so hear me out on it. God is real, so is Jesus. He created you and has plans for you. Life's a lot bigger than what you see right now."

"Hey! Don't preach at me. I know what's right and wrong; I got a good mama. My daddy went to church before, well, you know. But here's how it is. Tonight is the big night. T Max has it all set up. We're gonna hit it big tonight, then after that, more. I could be set for life.

It wouldn't be this tired, old neighborhood anymore. I'd be somebody and I'd take care of Mama, too."

I sat back down, leaned back and stretched a bit.

"Tré, I know you think you've got this figured out, but you're wrong. I know. I spent time in prison, a long time. I got there because I did what you just described; the drug scene, using and selling. I lived the life you want to have."

I paused to see how he was taking it. He was listening, so I pressed ahead.

"When you do that, you live on the run, knowing that at the next town the police are going to get you. You think T Max and Quince are your friends? Listen to me. They aren't. They'll turn and run, leaving you to face the police or die. If you don't end up dead before the age of twenty, you'll be angry, afraid and restless until the day they arrest you. Then they'll lock you behind razor wire and bars and you'll live out your days in a concrete cell no bigger than your bedroom in this house. You'll be all alone, trusting no one and, if you're lucky, you'll die early. That's the life you want, Tré? You're fifteen years old. You're smart. God loves you. You've got a whole lot of people that love you and believe in you. As I see it, you got two choices. You can hang with the likes of T Max and Quince. If you do, you'll end up where I did or like your dad did. Your other choice is to do the hard thing, the right thing. Turn your back on that lifestyle and trust that God offers you better. I guess that's what I had to say. That's it."

Again, I looked at Tré. He didn't look angry. It seemed like he was listening.

"You been in prison, old man? For real?"

"Yeah, Tré. Just got out."

"I believe you, old man. You knew my dad, huh? So, what do I do? I heard all that you said. I'm not saying I'll do anything different, but suppose I do. What do you want me to do?"

I smiled.

"What I want you to do is real simple. Don't go with T Max and Quince tonight. Stay here with your mom. Do whatever the two of you do. I don't care. Just don't go."

He contemplated my request.

"I don't know. I'd be giving up a lot. T Max would likely throw me out. I'd be risking…"

"You wanted to know, so I told you. Hey, just do it, tonight. Do it for an old guy who knew your dad. Do it for yourself."

"Don't go?"

"Yeah, that's it. You'll understand later."

"You sure?"

"Yeah, I'm positive."

***

I LEFT Tré and walked over to Yolanda's house. I climbed the porch steps. Before I knocked on the door, I felt my face, rubbed my jaw and checked to see if my mouth was still bleeding. I hadn't been in a fight like that for years. After determining that I was presentable, I knocked. The door creaked open and Yolanda stood there as she had before. I looked back to see if Tré was still on the porch, but he was gone. The house looked vacant.

"Come in, Greg," Yolanda told me. "How are you?"

"Well, I won't lie. I've been better," I told her, "but I'm all right. I talked with Tré. I think you'll know the answer to what I'm about to ask. Did he go? What happened?"

Yolanda took my hand and pulled me to the couch. I sat. Sun-Hi was sitting in the rocker next to the window.

"I want you to see this, Greg. It's the paper Sun-Hi brought to me. You remember, don't you?"

"Yeah, sure I do. It's the one with the article about the teen being shot. It quoted you talking about what a tragedy it was that Tré had died. You read it to me."

"Read it yourself."

"Why? You already read it to me. Why don't you just answer my question?"

"Please. Read it."

I took the paper and looked under the fold. The article just under the fold had a headline that said, "Two Arrested in Hamilton County." I looked up at Yolanda and Sun-Hi, puzzled. I then read some more. "Terrance Maxwell and Quincy DeAngelo were arrested for possession with the intent to sell…" It didn't say anything about a teen getting shot. I looked up at Yolanda again.

"What does this mean? It doesn't say anyone was shot or died."

"It means he didn't go, Greg. Praise the Lord! You did it."

I leaned back on the couch, closed my eyes and said a prayer of thanks. I knew it was a miracle.

"Oh man, that's amazing. What happened to Tré and

his mom? Tell us, Yolanda. We'd really like to know."

There was no reply.

"Come on," I said, "don't leave me hanging…"

I opened my eyes. I was on the couch in the living room and Sun-Hi was still in the rocking chair. The room was exactly the same, except Yolanda was gone. I turned to Sun-Hi.

"What happened? Where did she go?"

Sun-Hi stood and took my hand.

"Come on, Greg. It's time for us to go."

Chapter Ten

Sun-Hi climbed into the Jeep and fastened her seat belt. I opened the driver's side door, and paused to look around the neighborhood. I wondered how many stories were blowing around Garden Terrace.

"Are we leaving?" Sun-Hi asked from the passenger seat.

"Yeah, I guess."

I climbed in, started the Jeep and backed out of the drive. In a few minutes we were back on the highway. Neither of us said anything. I was still trying to process all that had just happened. I pulled over on the shoulder of the highway, though it wouldn't have mattered if I'd stopped in the middle of the road. No one was around.

"Sun-Hi, I don't know how much more I can do. That encounter with Tré McKinnick was hard, in more ways than one. I'm not saying I won't do more. I understand this isn't about me, but I need to rest a bit. I'm starting to feel, I don't know, tired, maybe. So, what's next?"

"Greg, I don't think there are any more encounters."

"Then, it's back to Lucasville? Is this it?"

"No, there is one more stop. We have to go to Ashton."

"Huh, why there? I've never been there. I don't know anyone from there."

She started to answer, but I interrupted.

"Okay, I don't have to know why. To Ashton it is."

I put the Jeep back into drive and in a matter of minutes we were back on interstate 71, headed north to the little town of Ashton.

✳✳✳

ASHTON was just a tiny dot on the state map of Ohio. It was about twelve miles north of Delhart. It had been, for all of its life, a simple farming community. The town square, if it could be called that, consisted of four buildings. There was a small grocery store, a city office building and courthouse, a convenience store and a locally owned feed and seed which had been there longer than the rest. Just to the south of the town square and a couple of blocks over was the only church in town: Ashton Community Church. The simple building had been used for a couple of other purposes throughout its history. Now, on any given Sunday, less than a hundred of the faithful gathered there for worship. A lot of the Godly folks in Ashton made the trip down the highway to a bigger church in the city. The town was slowly losing steam as more people moved away than came in.

Farming had always been rough, but in the last few years the economic downturn really hit Ashton. What crops could be sold were sold for very little. For a number of farmers it was just as profitable to let the fields lay fallow and not plant and harvest, though no one ever liked doing that. Retirees visited the town square each morning for coffee at the convenience store. There wasn't much commerce in the downtown area and the few children that lived here were bussed south to school. Ashton had never been a really big or significant place and now it was nothing more than another slumbering, dying town in central Ohio.

***

WE saw the sign for the Ashton exit and I slowed a little. I turned onto the country highway that would become Main Street in Ashton. A few minutes later I parked the Jeep next to the convenience store. As I expected, there were no cars and no people.

"Here we are," I said to Sun-Hi as I put the Jeep in park and turned off the ignition. "What's the plan?"

"Greg, I think he wants to see you now."

"Who does," I replied, "Sun-Hi, what are you talking about?"

Sun-Hi had already got out of the Jeep, though, and was running down the abandoned street.

"Come on, Greg."

I hurried to catch up with her and finally did just outside of the church.

"Now hold on," I demanded, "What are you talking about? Who wants to see me?"

Sun-Hi took my hand and started pulling me toward the front door of the church.

"You'll see, Greg, you'll see."

We got to the doors and as I pulled, they creaked open. The small windows in the foyer and the setting sun outside combined to create an odd, shadowy darkness in the church. The sanctuary windows were shuttered, making it nearly impossible to see into it at all. I groped for the light switch, but Sun-Hi didn't wait. She ran across the foyer and into the small, humble sanctuary. It took me a few seconds, but I finally found the switch. I flipped it, but nothing happened.

"Sun-Hi," I called out to her. "Where are you?"

I heard movement in the sanctuary. It had to be Sun-Hi.

"Come on, kid. This isn't funny."

I walked slowly up the center aisle, using the edges of the pews as a handrail. At last I came to the pew where Sun-Hi was.

"Why didn't you say anything?" I chided her. "It's really dark in here. Now that I found you, let's find some light and then we can talk about what you said earlier."

"We won't need to, Greg," she answered.

"Huh," I replied. "What are you trying to say?"

At that moment a light exploded in the sanctuary. I'd never seen anything so bright. It seemed white hot in intensity, yet combined every color of the rainbow. I fell to the floor with my face to the threadbare carpet. I became painfully aware that I was in the presence of a powerful, incredible and perfect being. My own imperfections were magnified in this pure light. Without having to hear a word from Sun-Hi, I knew I was in the presence of the Lord Jesus Christ himself. I began to weep. Tears of sadness, regret, sinful actions; all of these were mixed as I lay in the center aisle of the old church.

"Greg, no more tears. I've heard your plea. I was there when you pledged your life to me as a boy. I was there when you called out to me today when you were stabbed. I've allowed Sun-Hi and others to interact with you in unusual ways so that you would have one last chance to do something significant. Greg, you did it. I am proud of you. Well done, faithful servant. Stand."

As he said that, he reached out and took my hand. I looked up at him for the first time. His dark hair was long and flowing. He had rugged features and an engaging smile. What stood out to me most, though, were his eyes; bright, shining as if light radiated from inside him.

"Greg, I'm sure that you have a lot of questions about what happens to Sara, Tré and how things worked out for all of them."

I stood and nodded. Sun-Hi had taken her place beside me, staring in wonder at the Lord whose glory filled the little sanctuary.

"I will show you what happens next because I have one last thing for you to do before you go back."

One more thing?

I started to ask about what it might be, but he reached out to take both of us by the hand and in that instant we were moved into a place that words fail to describe. We were taken to heaven. It was that fast and just that simple. The beauty and perfection of heaven is astounding. An amazing sense of calm came over me. It was as if the pressures and problems of the world no longer existed. Time was of no consequence. I'd never been in such a place.

"Come here, Greg," Jesus called out to me. "I need to show you some things. I think this will answer your questions."

Sun-Hi and I moved nearer to Jesus Christ. As we

did, we began to see what I have no doubt he always sees; time past, time present and time future.

"Look now, Greg," he urged me. "Concentrate on Sara."

I did and I saw her getting out of the green Ranger and hugging Grant Swisher. It all began to unfold. I saw it as if it was a movie on the big screen.

**

SARA pulled into the drive at the Swisher's and as she opened the door, Grant came out, lumbered down the porch steps and embraced her in a bear hug. Sara buried her head in his shoulders and wept. She wept for Frances, Grant, Nancy, Grace; for all of them. Mostly she cried for herself. She had taken so much for granted. Frances emerged from the house. She'd been crying, but had found strength in comforting her family. She walked up to Sara, who released Grant. Sara could only smile a bit through her tears.

"Come here," Frances reached out to her. "It's gonna be all right. You know he loved you like you were part of the family."

"I know," Sara stammered.

"Now listen. It's hard to accept, but we know where George is and none of us here would wish him back. Not today. Not tomorrow. Not ever. Come inside, Sara. We've got plenty of food and lots of things to discuss."

**

THE scene disappeared and another began to form. It was in a church; George's funeral. The Swisher family was there and right in the middle of them sat Sara. She'd bought a new dress. She was crying, but not in a desperate, hopeless way. They were the tears of missing someone who'd become part of the fabric of day to day life. I heard Sara speaking after the service.

"George was like a father or a grandfather to me. I know he prayed for me, every day. Yeah, preacher, I'll be back on Sunday. You can count on it."

***

I SMILED. I started to say something, but was interrupted. A large hand rested on my shoulder. I turned to look.

"George!"

I don't know why I was shocked, after all, I knew where he was and I had just seen him, but his presence here was still surprising.

"Good job, Greg, you and Sun-Hi."

I stood to face George. He didn't look old anymore. His face didn't show any signs of aging, nor did he seem to be overweight. I knew it was George, but he looked like, I don't know, a "perfect" George.

"Hey, I want to thank you for the advice you gave. You were right. Thank you, too, for loving Sara and praying for her. I guess you already know the difference you made."

He smiled.

"I sure am pleased with that kid, that's for sure."

I heard Jesus speak once again.

"Focus again, Greg."

As I did, another scene played out before me.

✳✳✳

IT was the church again, but this time it wasn't a funeral. There were flowers, bows, ribbons and the people were dressed elegantly. I saw Frances Swisher there, sitting with Nancy. Nancy and Grant's kids were there. I saw Grace next to Frances. Grace's husband and kids were there, too. I saw some people standing at the front of the church. They were all guys, dressed in suits. A wedding! Then I saw her. Sara was dressed in a stunning gown. Grant Swisher was escorting her down the aisle. Sara was getting married! I watched as the service took place. There is no concept of time in heaven. The preacher asked Sara's future husband, who I found out was named Josh, if he would take Sara to be his lawful wife. I heard him ask Sara if she would take this man to be her husband. She said her "I do," loud and clear. I heard him ask, "Who is giving this woman?" and Grant spoke up, "Her family and I." I looked again at Sara. She had the biggest smile I'd ever seen. She was happy.

✳✳✳

THE scene shifted again. I saw Sara and Josh together. They were sitting in an office. Sara's smile was gone. Josh looked confused and nervous. A man in a white coat was speaking.

"We have the test results back."

"Okay, doctor," Josh said, his voice cracking just a bit, "what do they say?"

The doctor looked down at his desk and sighed. I knew the news wasn't going to be good.

"I'm sorry. The results are negative. Sara, I'm afraid

you won't be able to have any children. I'm truly sorry. The damage to your body over the years has made you infertile. I know that's not what you wanted to hear. I wish I had better news."

I saw Josh gulp and quickly grab Sara's hand. Sara dissolved into tears. The doctor quietly stood and told Josh that he'd allow them a few minutes of privacy.

"It's my fault," Sara cried as she pulled away from Josh. "I abused my body for so long that I've destroyed any chance we have at a family. Oh Josh! I'm so sorry."

Josh reached for her even as she tried to pull away.

"No, Sara. It's not your fault. It just is what it is. If God means for us to have children, we will."

***

THE scene dissolved and almost instantly another one came into focus. It was a bright, sunny day. I looked and saw the Swisher brood. They were all standing next to a big, Ford truck loaded with boxes in the back. A small moving truck was parked next to the Ford. Sara, Frances, Grace and Nancy stood together beside the Ford. Josh, Grant and Grace's husband, Will, were next to the moving truck.

"I sure wish you didn't have to move," Frances said.

"It's going to be challenging, but the promotion Josh was offered is too good."

"It's going to be roughest on the kids," Nancy chimed in. "All our kids love Aunt Sara and Uncle Josh. You'll be missed."

Sara seemed to be choking back tears.

"We'll miss all of you, too. Dayton's not that far,

though. You all can come up to visit. We'll be back here, too. This place will always be home. We'll visit."

"You'd better," Frances chimed in. "Be sure to call. Let us know what's going on. Don't forget."

"We won't."

After a few more good-byes, the Ford and the moving truck drove away from Delhart.

✽✽✽

THE scene dissolved again and in its place I could only hear voices. It was like I was overhearing a phone call.

"That's right, Nancy. Our lawyer called last night with the news. We're on the list to get a child."

"Oh my! Praise the Lord. We've been praying. Mom will be so excited. Tell me again how all of this happened."

✽✽✽

THE voices were gone. I stood with the Lord and Sun-Hi.

"Thank you," I started.

"Greg, there's more you need to see."

"Tré?"

Jesus smiled.

Chapter Eleven

"Focus your mind on Tré."

I did and the scenes, as they had with Sara's life, began to unfold from Tré's.

✻✻✻

Tré got up from the porch. I recognized him and the setting. This was just after I'd spoken with him; right after our fight. He went to the bathroom in his house and looked closely at his eye. He was starting to get a good shiner. I must've thrown a pretty good punch. He took off his shirt and I realized again that he was a lot like his dad. His muscles were evident. This was not the body of a boy. He was a strong man. Once again, I questioned my sanity in taking him on. He looked at the bruises on his shoulders and the scrapes on his back and on his head. He'd been in a fight, but he'd heal. I watched him put on his shirt. He went back into the kitchen. I saw the clock on the wall. If he was going to leave, it would have to be in the next few minutes. He took out his phone. It looked like he might send a text to someone. He started one, but then stopped. He started again, but stopped again.

Finally, he tossed the phone on the kitchen table. He lumbered into the living room and went to the bookshelf. He pulled out a book, an album. I saw as he looked through the old family photos. I lost track of time or of what else was happening. A door creaked open. JoAnne entered the house through the kitchen.

"Tré, you're home? I thought you said you had a party or something."

Tré stood and walked over to his mom. He hugged her. She seemed surprised.

"Nah, Mom, I think I'll just hang around here. Is that okay?"

JoAnne stepped away from his embrace.

"Of course, I can fix something for dinner."

"No, I got a little money. Let me take you out."

JoAnne smiled.

"Well, isn't that something. I'd be honored to accompany you."

***

ANOTHER scene immediately became visible. JoAnne was in the kitchen. She was making breakfast; nothing special, just breakfast. As she poured orange juice, Tré came in with his phone. He was visibly shaken.

"Mom, I need to tell you something."

JoAnne turned from the counter.

"What is it?"

"I just got a text. Terrance and Quincy got arrested."

JoAnne didn't seem surprised, but didn't want to show it.

"I'm sorry to hear that."

"No, you don't understand. I was supposed to be with them last night. I was supposed to be there. I wasn't because, well, I just wasn't. It could've been me, Mom. I could be in some dirty jail this morning instead of here."

"But you're not, Tré."

"I know, but I could be; maybe should be."

Tré pulled up a website on his computer. It had pictures of the arrested young men; Terrance Maxwell and Quincy DeAngelo.

"My picture could be there. Right there! Things have got to change. They will. I promise."

***

THE kitchen vanished and a different scene came into focus. It was a high school gymnasium. Chairs were in rows. People were dressed up. Graduation. I looked closely. I saw Yolanda Dennison. Her hair was still gray, but it was neatly combed. She wore a light blue dress and was sitting at the end of a row. She clutched a camera. Right next to her was JoAnne McKinnick. I heard the familiar graduation music and the graduates proceeded forward. I scanned the crowd of grads, looking for Tré. I didn't see him. Then I looked on the stage. There he was, seated next to two other grads and other dignitaries. The ceremony began with an invocation. The principal spoke and introduced everyone. She said a few words and then introduced the salutatorian to come and give his speech.

"It is my pleasure to introduce to you our class salutatorian, Walter McKinnick III."

I saw Tré stand. People were applauding. Yolanda snapped pictures as fast as she could. JoAnne wiped tears from her eyes. Tré placed his notes on the podium and started.

"Fellow graduates, parents, friends and dignitaries. It is an honor for me to stand here tonight to represent this class. We're all here tonight to celebrate our success. However, we should not forget the sacrifices and the hard work of others that allowed us to enjoy this night. I personally want to thank my mom and my dad, who died when I was a small boy, for the sacrifices they made. I didn't always get it then, but I do now. The greatest contribution we make to our family and society is when we give of ourselves, even if it goes unnoticed."

His speech continued for another six minutes to fill his allotted time. It was pretty clear to me that he'd kept the promise he made at the kitchen table the day after our fight.

✳✳✳

GRADUATION faded and in its place another event came into focus. It was a party; no a reception. It was at the house in Terrace Gardens. Yolanda was there, looking a bit older. Some of the other neighbors were there, too. I saw JoAnne. She had aged gracefully. She seemed happier than I'd seen her.

"Look, they're coming," a little girl who lived in the neighborhood called out.

"All right everyone," Yolanda instructed. "Get ready."

The door opened and Tré entered with a young lady on his arm.

"Surprise!"

Tré and the young lady seemed surprised.

"What's all this?" he asked.

118

"It's a party," Yolanda called out. "It isn't every day that someone from Terrace Gardens graduates law school."

"Don't forget about the engagement," someone called out from the back.

"That's right," JoAnne said as she moved to hug Tré and his fiancé. "My family is growing. This is the happiest I've been in a long time. Congratulations, both of you."

✶✶✶

THE celebration faded much faster than I wanted. An office came into view. Tré was at a conference table with two other men. He spoke to them.

"I know we have several pro-bono opportunities here. I'm not saying they aren't worthy or important, but I've become aware of a program that has touched me deeply. It helps Americans adopt foreign orphans. My church hosted an event and a representative spoke. I met with him after the conference and asked for this meeting."

"Just what are you hoping for, Walter?" the oldest of the two men asked.

"I'd like to offer legal services to the families that want to utilize this program. Adoptions, especially foreign ones, are expensive and require specialized legal work. I'd like to offer my services for that. I think others might, too."

"It's an interesting idea," the younger of the two noted. "Is all the information about the program in this file?"

"Yes sir."

"Good," the older one replied. "We'll check it over

and get back with you."

The meeting appeared to be headed for a quick ending. The younger man, though, had a question.

"If you don't mind me asking, Walter, why do this? We have plenty of options for charity work. Why foreign born adoptions? It seems, I don't know, kind of random."

Tré smiled.

"I suppose I have a heart for kids who don't have parents. If there are people that are really wanting to love and parent kids and there are kids that need parents, it seems the least I can do is to help them through the legal hurdles. I suppose it's a way that I can give to God and to people who can't give back to me. Sacrifice is important, right?"

The two partners nodded.

"Thank you both for your time. I'll await your answer."

The older man smiled.

"We'll look it over, but you made a good case, counselor. I think you can probably go ahead and set up this program."

***

THE men stood and shook hands. The scene vanished. I'd hoped to see more.

"Wait," I called out. "What happened to Tré's program?"

I was interrupted by a tugging on my shirt. I turned and saw her. Her hair was no longer gray and she didn't have those crazy wire-rimmed glasses. Like George was still George, Yolanda was still Yolanda, but she was a "perfect" Yolanda.

"He turned out real good, Greg."

"Huh," I asked.

"You asked me a question a while back. I wanted to answer it. He turned out real good."

I smiled.

"He sure did."

"He married that girl. Denae was her name. I guess you just saw that he's a lawyer. He was hired by a big firm in Dayton. He got the message, too. I've never seen anyone so dedicated to the Lord, his family or doing for others. He bought a house on the east side and JoAnne moved into an apartment they had built for her in the house. It was hard for her to move from Terrace Gardens, but she needed to go. Denae and Walter have four children. She helps Denae with the kids. Still does."

"That's great," I said. "He has done well."

Jesus touched me on the shoulder.

"Greg, that's what I needed to show you."

"I get it now, Lord. I understand. The little things that we don't even think about can change everything."

I turned to see if Yolanda would back me up on that, but she was gone.

"One act does more than the doer knows, that's for sure."

"I haven't said this yet, but I want to. Thank you. Thank you for not giving up on me. Thank you for hearing my cry. I am more grateful and humbled than I ever have been."

I stopped.

"Lord, you don't suppose that I could…"

Before I could finish the sentence, he turned and smiled. I saw her and began to cry. Mom.

"You did it, Greg. I'm proud of you. Love you more than you'll ever know."

I hugged my mom tightly. She no longer looked tired, old and beaten down. She was as pretty as I remembered her being when I was a boy.

"It wasn't easy, Mom, but it feels good to know I've finally done something right."

She continued to hug me as she replied, "I know, Son."

I pulled back a bit from her embrace.

"Mom, what about Amber? I know she's here."

"She sure is. She's a beautiful young lady, now. Perfect in every way."

"She's not hurting, then?"

"Not one time since the day she got here."

"I'd sure like to see her."

"You will."

I smiled and bowed my head. As I looked up, my mom was gone. Jesus stood before me again.

"Greg, here's the last thing I want you to do."

I looked as intently as one can look at the face of perfection.

"You and Sun-Hi will be back in the little church in just a moment. You'll be by yourselves there. I want you to write your story. Tell everything that has happened this day."

"Why?"

"Your story will be a lesson and a reminder to others.

It's never too late to call out to me. I desperately want people to come to me and spend eternity in heaven. You have got to make it clear. It's never too late. You need to tell them that. Also, they need to know to not put off doing the things that matter. The small things that seem to make no difference can have great consequence. Write your story, Greg. Tell them."

As he said that, the magnificent light that had defined his essence was swooshed up. Sun-Hi and I were no longer in heaven. We found ourselves back in the little sanctuary of the community church. It was dark again.

"I guess you know what to do," Sun-Hi told me.

I turned to her and noticed the computer there in the pew.

"I do."

Sun-Hi sat down next to me as I opened the computer and turned it on. In seconds it was ready. I paused. How do I put into words what I'd just experienced? Sun-Hi noticed my hesitation.

"Just tell it like it happened."

I smiled.

Yep. That's what I should do, all right.

I then began typing the words, "My name is Greg McBride, but for the last thirty years I've been known by the state of Ohio as #311572. That was my prison…"

I'd worked on the story for what seemed like a long time. I looked over at Sun-Hi who sat quietly on the pew next to me.

"It's been quite a day, huh?"

She smiled and nodded.

"Hey Sun-Hi, as I've been writing this, something's

kind of been bothering me. I should've asked about it sooner, but I didn't think of it until now. What is your role in all of this? I guess I'm asking what's in this for you."

She smiled again.

"I don't know, Greg."

"Come on, kid, I'm not buying that."

"Finish writing, Greg."

I returned to pecking away at the keyboard. As I did, I felt a sharp pain. My neck really hurt. It wasn't just a writer's cramp. I'd experienced some pain during the fight with Tré, but that pain seemed a bit muted. This really hurt.

"Wow, Sun-Hi! My neck's hurting. I don't think it's a cramp. I haven't hurt like this since, well, since I got stabbed."

Sun-Hi stood.

"Greg, we have to go now."

"Hold on. I'm not finished yet. Surely I'll get enough time to finish."

"Bring the computer. We have to leave now."

Sun-Hi grabbed my hand. She was more insistent than she had been throughout the whole day.

"All right. I'm coming."

I saved what I had written and shut down the computer. I carried the computer to the door of the church. As we stepped through the door, I felt another sharp pain in my neck. Instinctively I put my hand at the point of the pain. When I looked down at it, I noticed a drop of blood. Sun-Hi saw it, too.

"Hurry, Greg."

We ran to the Jeep and climbed in. Sun-Hi took the computer from me and opened it. She also put in a flash drive that had been in the case.

"You can dictate to me and I'll type what you say. I'll save it on this."

I started the Jeep and backed away from the church and drove down Main Street in Ashton. It wasn't long before we were back on the highway, headed south to Lucasville.

"Okay, Greg," Sun-Hi said. "Tell me more of the story. What's next?"

I tried to continue the story. My mind wasn't as clear, though, as it had been. The pain was more intense and more frequent.

"I'll try, Sun-Hi."

I remembered what I could. The words were coming out slower and the images in my mind were fading. We neared Lucasville, where this journey had begun earlier.

"We're almost there, Greg. You're doing great," Sun-Hi encouraged me.

"I gotta stop for a minute, kid," I said as I leaned over the steering wheel. "I need some air. I can't breathe."

I pulled over just a few miles from the entrance to the Southeast Ohio Correctional Facility. Sun-Hi jumped out of the Jeep and ran around it to my side. I opened the door and stepped down. When I did, she gasped and took a step back. I was back in my orange prison issue clothes. My neck was bleeding more heavily, staining the orange shirt I was wearing. She grabbed me.

"Greg, hurry. There isn't much time."

She pushed me back into the Jeep. I took a deep

breath, as deep a one as I could, and turned the ignition. I jammed the Jeep into drive and pulled out onto the road. I weaved back and forth on both sides of the highway approaching the turn. As had been the case every time, no other cars were around. We finally came to the prison entrance. I turned. The pain was becoming more than I could bear. I was no longer able to verbalize my story. My thoughts were elsewhere. *Jesus! Please. Help me. Forgive me.* I rolled the Jeep to a stop in the parking lot. Sun-Hi jumped from the Jeep, ran to the other side and opened my door for me. I could barely move. She pulled me from the Jeep and, somehow, I was still able to stand and walk. She held my hand as we walked through the empty lobby area. As we had earlier, we easily got through the metal detectors and the heavy steel door. She held me as we walked by the guard station and through the door into the yard. The sun was still shining brightly.

"Keep going, Greg. You're almost there."

"Sun-Hi," I spoke haltingly, as words were hard to form and speak. "Sun-Hi, I still don't know about you."

"No time, Greg," she replied quickly.

"But the story," I whispered.

"Don't worry, Greg. I'll make sure it's finished. I promise."

We were back at the chapel now. I could see people standing around. They weren't moving. They were like statues. We'd walked through here before. It all seemed eerily familiar. As Sun-Hi pulled the door of the chapel open, the sky grew dark. It began raining, hard. She pulled me through. I began to hear voices, urgent voices, speaking. I looked to Sun-Hi, but she was starting to fade away.

"No," I tried to cry out in what came out as a whisper. "Please Lord. Jesus, let me know about Sun-Hi. Jesus, please. Jesus."

I was back on the floor of the chapel. My prison issue was wet and sticky with blood. I tried to call out to the Lord, but there was no more breath. The pain became excruciating. I heard the medics say something about "losing him." Then, the pain was gone.

Chapter Twelve

There was chaos in the chapel at the prison. Inmates were shouting. Guards were doing their best to clear the room. Dempsey and Big Tony had escaped through the crowd and confusion; at least for the moment. The chaplain and a small group of inmates finished a prayer, then the chaplain led them out. The medics who had come just after the stabbing were still kneeling around the lifeless body of Greg McBride.

"Who noted the time of death for the death certificate?"

"I got it," a woman called out. "He died at 10:52 a.m."

"Did somebody call the doctor?"

"Yeah, he's on the way."

"What about the warden?"

"Yep, he's already here. He's outside talking to Hughes about what happened and who did it."

"Where do we put the body?"

"Don't know for sure. Usually the warden makes that contact, unless there's an autopsy."

A man put a sheet over Greg's face, covering the

wound in his neck. The blood on the front of his orange shirt was still visible just below the sheet.

"Here comes Anderson, one of the assistant admins. Let's ask him about the body."

"I'll stay here and wait."

Three members of the medical team walked through the door to check with Anderson. One waited.

✻✻✻

THERE wasn't an autopsy performed. The cause of death was apparent. He'd died because his carotid artery had been severed. He bled to death. The bigger question was who did it. The press came out and interviewed the warden and the chaplain. An internal investigation was launched. None of the inmates had much interest in cooperating. None of them seemed to see anything. No one really missed Greg McBride. There was no public demand for justice for the murder of a murderer. The media did not find the story fascinating, so after the initial report in the local news, nothing was said. His body was picked up by the Garret and Sons Funeral Home. He'd be held in their morgue, as had many others, until family came to get him. If they didn't come in forty-eight hours, he'd be buried in the state cemetery not far from the prison. The article noting his death was in the June 13, 2013 edition of the local paper. Papers around the state of Ohio picked it up and ran it in the "regional news" section the next day.

✻✻✻

THERE was a lot of noise in the cafeteria of Eastside High School just outside of Dayton. For many of the students, this was one of the better parts of the day. One young lady, though, was not as excited about spending time in that "circus." Every chance she had to have lunch at a different location, she jumped on it. When the librarian offered students the opportunity to eat in the library where they could read and study, she eagerly volunteered. Her academic performance and her behavior in class made her an easy pick. She hurried to get a lunch tray to escape the madness of the cafeteria for the calm of the library.

"Hey, are you eating in the library today? I was going to save you a seat in here."

"Yes, but thanks anyway, Beth," she replied to her friend.

She hurried down the hall and entered the library. She found an empty table and sat down with her tray. Normally she would work on homework, which didn't take very long. Sometimes she would read a book. Today, though, she saw the newspapers on the rack and grabbed one. It was the Dayton paper. Very few high school kids have much interest in a newspaper, and those who do are usually into fashion or sports. She, however, scanned the front page and then flipped it open to the local and regional news. As she glanced through the articles there, she gasped. The librarian lifted her head and reminded everyone to be quiet. The girl looked down again and read through the paragraph another time.

"That can't be!"

The librarian was standing now.

"Sun-Hi, if you can't be quiet, you'll have to return to the cafeteria."

Sun-Hi quickly looked down.

"I'm sorry," she replied.

She finished her lunch quietly. She folded the paper, but didn't put it back on the rack. She hid it in her backpack. She couldn't wait to get home.

***

HOME, according to Sun-Hi, was one of the nicest words in the English language. She'd learned English and Korean, her native tongue, at the orphanage. She'd been brought there as a baby by a mother who'd already had more kids than she could handle. She grew up in that orphanage. She prayed every day for a family. By the time she was twelve years old, though, no one had come for her. No one seemed to want her. She thought she'd never get to have a family or a home, so she considered running away from the orphanage. It wasn't a terrible place, but she was desperate to find someone of her own. That's what she wanted more than anything; a family and a home. She'd just about decided to do it, when she was called into the office. An American lawyer had called the orphanage. He was working for a couple that was interested in adopting her. No wonder she'd been given so many tests lately. The administrator told her that they would be coming to visit. She was so excited at the possibility, that she ran, hugged the administrator and cried into his shirt.

***

AFTER the brief conversation with the administrator of the orphanage in Seoul, Walter hung up and called the couple with whom he had been working.

"Hey, how are you doing? Yes. Good. I just got off

the phone with him in Korea. The child we spoke of earlier passed the health tests. I know. I'm excited, too. Don't be ashamed to cry. It's a happy time. Absolutely. She's twelve now. I don't know when we can make this final, but yes. Tell Josh that you're going to need to go to South Korea. Check flights. She knows you're coming. I'm sure she's excited. Yes, I do know her name. It's Sun-Hi."

✻✻✻

THE first meeting took place at the orphanage in Seoul. Josh and Sara were a bit nervous as they met the orphanage representative at the airport. He carried their luggage to the car. They walked behind him and talked in hushed tones.

"Josh," Sara said, "what if she doesn't want to go with us? What if she hates us? I couldn't bear that thought. I've prayed for a child for so long. I know you have, too. Please tell me this is going to work."

"Sara, come on. Relax. We've prayed and know that God's in charge. You've taught me that more than anyone I know. What do they say, 'Physician heal thyself' well, you've talked about trusting, do it."

"I know, I just want this so badly. I love her already. I hope she'll be open to us."

They arrived at the orphanage and entered. The administrator met them and led them to a "meeting room." A few moments later, a beautiful twelve-year old Korean girl meekly entered the room. She sat down in the chair opposite Sara and Josh.

"Are you here for me?" she timidly asked in her best

English.

Tears pouring down her face, Sara replied, "Yes, Sun-Hi. We're here for you. We want to be your family."

***

"Home" became Dayton. On this particular day, Sun-Hi could hardly wait to get there. She got off the bus and ran down the block to her house. She opened the screen door at the back of the house that led to the kitchen.

"Mom," she called out. "Mom! Where are you?"

Sun-Hi was a freshman in high school. She rarely acted like a kid so her exuberance startled Sara.

"Up here. What do you need, Sun-Hi? Are you okay?"

Sun-Hi ran up the stairs and practically plowed into her mother who was coming out of the upstairs guest room. She dropped her backpack and pulled the newspaper from the side pocket. She thrust it at Sara.

"Mom, you need to read this."

"What's that, dear? What do I need to read?"

Sun-Hi was becoming impatient.

"This," she exclaimed as she pointed to the small paragraph. "Read it while I go get something."

Sara scanned the paragraph. It was about an inmate who'd been killed in the southern part of the state. Why would Sun-Hi care about that? Sun-Hi burst out of her room holding a flash drive.

"Mom, I knew it. I did it. I did it. I kept it so long. But I'm so glad I did. Here it is."

She was holding the flash drive, but Sara was still struggling to understand what any of this meant.

"Why don't we just go downstairs, sit in the kitchen

and talk a bit more."

"Yeah, that's a good idea, Mom."

Sun-Hi bounded down the stairs and Sara followed, still bewildered by her normally calm and composed daughter's sudden venture into crazy. Sun-Hi was already in the kitchen when Sara entered.

"You'd better have a seat, Mom."

She'd already turned on her computer and was downloading whatever was on the flash drive.

"Hold on now," Sara replied. "I want some answers. What's going on with you? What's got you so fired up? What's this article got to do with anything and where did you get that flash drive?"

"Let me explain. I don't know if you'll believe me, Mom, but I hope you do. I have never lied to you before so please believe me now. You know that you and Dad got me from the orphanage in Seoul."

"Of course, Sun-Hi, but..." Sara started.

"Please let me finish, Mom," Sun-Hi implored. "I promise you'll get it when I'm finished."

She then continued.

"I went to that orphanage when I was just a baby. I don't really have any memories of my biological mother. I do remember a mission worker, though. She was a sweet, gentle lady. She worked with me at the orphanage and I think I became her special kid or whatever. One day, she pulled me aside. She told me that I was a precious gift. She told me God loved me and had plans for me. She also wanted me to have this flash drive. The one I just put into the computer. She said I wouldn't understand for a long time, but I would later. She wrote

134

a name on the flash drive. She told me when I saw that name, I should get that flash drive and give it to the woman who was my mother. I kept that flash drive in my treasure box for all these years. I'd even forgotten about the name on the flash drive, until today. Look, Mom."

She pulled the flash drive from the computer port and gave it to her mother. The name, though written a long time ago, was still clear. It said, "Greg McBride."

"That's who's in the article. When I read that today, something clicked. I remembered what I had put out of my mind so many years ago. Mom, I've not seen what's on this thing, but we're supposed to, I think."

Sara sat at her kitchen table. She stared at a computer screen that was ready to reveal the contents of a flash drive that her daughter was convinced they needed to see.

"I believe you, Sun-Hi. I don't know what this means or why this is happening, but I believe you. Let's see what's on here."

Sun-Hi clicked on the "View Download" icon. In moments a document flashed before them. They read the first words, "My name is Greg McBride, but for the last thirty years…" It took them more than two hours to complete the story. It ended with Greg and Sun-Hi at the prison.

"Mom," Sun-Hi began timidly, "Greg McBride is your dad. He's my grandpa, isn't he?"

"Sun-Hi, I don't know," Sara started, then stopped. "Yes, Sun-Hi, he is. Do you remember any of this, what's written here?"

Sun-Hi looked at her mother.

"No, Mom, I really don't."

"I don't remember meeting a Greg McBride either," Sara replied. "I remember some of the stuff written down here; some of it I wish you hadn't read, but I don't really recall meeting this guy."

"But do you think it happened? Because, Mom, I do. I don't know why but I do. There's more. I think we need to go down there to get him. He should be buried next to Amber in Euclid. I also think you're supposed to finish this."

Sara was shocked at her daughter's analysis.

"I agree with you about his body and him being buried. But I'm no writer. I wouldn't know what to say."

"You read what he wrote, finish it. Tell what happened. His story is supposed to be out there. It's supposed to be a reminder to people. Mom, he did a lot of bad things. I don't think anyone will disagree with that, but I think he did something good, too, for all of us; you, Dad, me, Walter. Finish his story."

***

Josh called the warden at the Southeast Ohio Correctional Facility in Lucasville that day. The warden was a bit surprised to hear from any family of Greg McBride, but he told Josh that they could contact the Garret and Sons Funeral Home. Josh spoke to the youngest Mr. Garret and arranged for the body to be delivered to a funeral home in Euclid. Sara did some research to find out where Amber McBride had been buried. Once she discovered that, she called and found out that there was a plot next to her grave. It hadn't been paid for, but Sara wasn't concerned about that. She agreed to the financial terms. She also contacted her minister who said he'd do the funeral. The service would be on Monday. Sara had one more call to make before she started packing.

"Hello, may I speak to Walter McKinnick please. Yes. I'll hold. Uh, yes. Sara Butler. Yes. Thank you."

"Hello, Sara, this is Walter. How are you?"

"I'm fine. We all are. Hey, I've got a strange request, but I've got to ask you. Do you remember a Greg McBride?"

There was silence on the other end. After a few seconds, Walter replied.

"Hmm, I don't think so. I can't recall it anyway."

"May I send you something to read? I know you're busy, but you should read it. Read it and get back with me, okay?"

"Sure, send it to me."

Sara emailed Greg's story and a few hours later the phone rang.

"Hello, Sara. I read it."

"Yeah, what do you think? Do you remember any of that?"

"To be honest Sara, I don't. At least I don't remember a Greg McBride. I can, unfortunately, verify the events he described in my life. It is absolutely true that I was part of a gang and was going to get a big score. I didn't go the night two others got arrested. From that point on, my life changed."

"Yeah," Sara told him, "same thing with me. All those things about drug use and selling are true. I did know a Michael and Manny. I was going to the Willard place. Those dumb things, like cows in the road, did happen."

"So, is it true?"

"I can't explain it, but I can't refute it either."

"What are you going to do?"

"We'll have the funeral in Euclid on Monday. Pastor Craig has already agreed to do it. We've got a plot there."

"What about the story?"

"Sun-Hi wants me to finish it."

"Will you?"

"I don't know."

***

THE Monday morning sky was bright and clear. It was already warm. Later, in the afternoon, the temperatures would reach near a hundred degrees. Sara, Josh and Sun-Hi came to the cemetery with Walter and Denae McKinnick. Pastor Craig and his wife arrived next. That was it. No one else was likely to come. Seven people gathered around a recently dug grave. The funeral home had erected a tent around the gravesite and set up a few folding chairs. A guest book sat on a stand, but it would go unused. The funeral director approached Sara at ten and asked if she wanted to wait a few more minutes to see if anyone else was coming. Sara politely declined and Pastor Craig began the service. He read a few Scriptures and had the small assembly there sing a hymn. He then spoke about faith in Jesus Christ. He told of how everyone sins, but it is grace that sets us free and provides us a pardon. He then did something that surprised Sara. He called Sun-Hi to share a few words. She stepped to the head of the casket and cleared her throat.

"I have tried desperately to remember the things my grandfather, Greg McBride, wrote about him and me in his story. I want to remember it. I do. The truth is, though, I don't. But here's what I do know. I know Greg got a chance in his last minute of life to correct some wrongs and to learn some things. I know he couldn't undo all that he'd done, but he did some good on that day. I know that he loved Jesus, even though he ignored him for most of his life. I also know that Jesus forgave him. I know it because Greg asked him to and that's what Jesus does. I know that Greg doesn't hurt any more, in any way. I know he got to see his granddaughter, though I don't think either of us realized it. I also know that he got to see his sister again in heaven. I'm proud to be his granddaughter. I know that sounds strange. The adopted girl is proud of her murderer grandfather. It sounds foolish, I know. But, I think I knew Greg McBride in a way most didn't. I can't explain it, but I believe it. Thank you, Greg. If you hadn't taken that one last chance, I'm sure I wouldn't be here today; maybe none of us would. His story has three important lessons. Remember, it is never too late to come to Jesus. Don't hesitate to do the little things because they matter. Last, always remember that Jesus loves you. Your life matters to him. So, again, thanks Grandpa. I hope things are good in heaven."

By the time she sat down next to her parents, all gathered there were in tears and Sara had decided she would finish the story.

Afterword

I, Sara Butler, completed this story. After my dad's funeral, I began writing about the events after Greg and Sun-Hi's return to Lucasville. I wrote from the middle of chapter eleven to what you're reading right now. I interviewed the chaplain and some of the inmates who agreed to talk to me. The "Introduction" is mine. I calculated his life to the minute. I thought that was a memorable way to highlight what happened in the last minute or so of his life here on earth. The account you find in between is what was on the flash drive. As I told you earlier, I can't verify that it happened. I have no way of knowing for sure. None of us in this story can recall specifically meeting Greg McBride. But I will say this; I believe it happened. I believe it occurred as it is portrayed in the preceding pages. The message of his story is clear. Sun-Hi said it well at his funeral. It's never too late to come to Jesus. Don't put off doing the little things because they can make a difference. Always know Jesus Christ loves you and that you are precious to him.

You can believe this story or not. That's up to you. I don't know if Greg's message will make a big impact on the world. I hope so, but that's not really what matters. I've tried to get it out there. I promised my daughter I would. She seems to think she promised my dad.

As an aside, you might be interested in knowing that Sun-Hi's name was given to her at birth. We didn't change it when we adopted her. We didn't try to "Americanize" it. It's who she is. In Korean, "Sun-Hi" means "goodness" or "joy." God has allowed her to bring that to Josh and me. I think she brought it to her grandfather, too.

—Sara Butler, Dayton, Ohio

Photo courtesy of TeAnne Chartrau

Bill Thomas lives in Washington, Missouri. He is the Christian Education Minister at First Christian Church and an adjunct instructor for Dallas Christian College. He's been the preaching minister at Stony Point Christian Church of Kansas City, Kansas and Northridge Church of Christ of Circleville, Ohio. He's also taught school in Kansas City, Kansas and Union, Missouri.

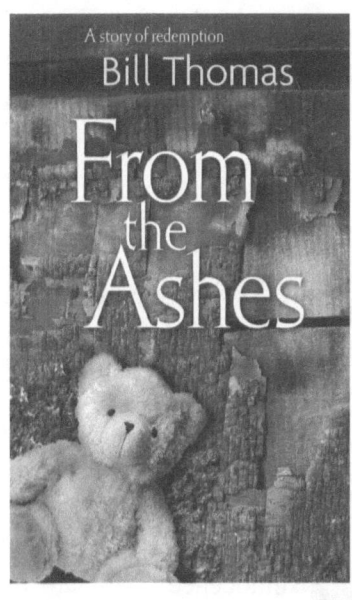

A story of redemption

Bill Thomas

From the Ashes

Jerold Volker was the youngest vice-president ever at one of Cincinnati's oldest and most prestigious banks. He was on the fast-track to success and he liked it. But Jerold had a secret – a deep, dark secret

– and he was soon to learn that secrets have a mind of their own. They want to be told. They want to see the light of day, no matter how hard you try to bury them. For Jerold, the past had latched onto his shirt-tail and followed him into the future, and now he must deal with it.

For Jerold, the secret came to him in the form of a mysterious text message that read simply "Help me". Frustrated and desperate, Jerold followed the clues back to his estranged Kentucky home town where the past quickly revealed itself.

But things are seldom as they seem, and soon Jerold was floundering in the ashes of his tortured past from which he'd so ardently fled.

Read this exciting, fast-moving thriller and grow with Jerold as he learns that pain and forgiveness are but two sides of the same coin; that the past cannot be buried and . . .

The secret will not be denied.

CHET HANSON

The **BUYER**

Leonard LaFrance only knows how to do one thing: make money…

You've likely never met anyone like Leonard: a titan of business, yet with an inexplicable innocence. Molded by his father to buy success at any cost, Leonard has been a faithful soldier—until one morning he finds it impossible to get out of bed. Paralyzed with despair, Leonard suddenly realizes that he doesn't know life at all. Determined to break out of his cocoon of security and unquestioned authority, he embarks on a journey of discovery. Along the way, Leonard finds he has the courage to change; to fall in love, and to earn a life worth living—to become more than just *The Buyer*.

Grateful Publishing ☺

Do you love chocolate? Do you love God? If the answer to both questions are "yes", then this book is for you. Whether you are a chocolate connoisseur or simply one who loves to bask in the rich aromas and flavors of the chocolate-enhanced life, you will love Becky Baxa's new book. *What Kind of Chocolate are You?* will go with you through the journey of becoming a mature Christian and be an inspiration to strengthen your faith; challenging you to new heights through the reflections into your soul, and inspiring you to be sweetly delicious to God and others.

White
Feather
Press

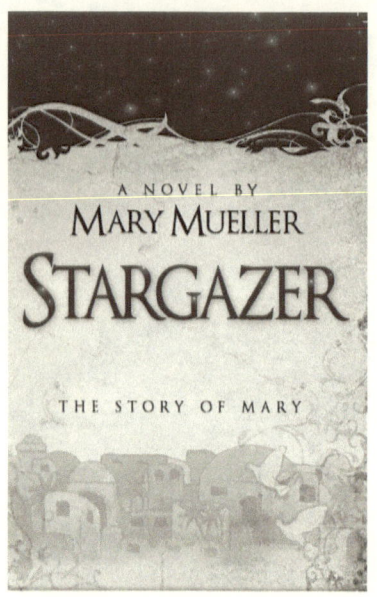

A NOVEL BY
MARY MUELLER

STARGAZER

THE STORY OF MARY

Mary Mueller brings a truly unique perspective of Mary the Mother of Jesus to life in the pages of *Stargazer*. I am struck by the number of new insights I gained into the life of our Lord and Savior Jesus Christ by reading about it through Mary's eyes. Mary tells this story adroitly and adeptly, with delightful turns of phrase and insightful facility of voice around every page turn. When we gaze into the stars, we see the glory of God; I believe readers will see His glory when they gaze into these pages as well!

— Mike Salsbury —
Actor, Author, and Artistic Director
Paraclete Productions
(www.paracleteproductions.net)

White
Feather
Press

He calls himself Accuser...and he knows your darkest secrets.

When Sara Thompson took the man's order, she had no idea he would take the entire diner hostage moments later. And she had no idea he would know her deepest, dirtiest sin. Calling himself Accuser, the man offers his victims a chance at freedom--but at a price. The Accuser's demand seems simple: All his captives have to do is reveal their blackest sins and they will walk free. But as one by one the hostages "testify," the game gets darker, and as Sara and the others are forced to face the shame of their pasts, the Accuser proves he knows more about his hostages than any of them can fathom.

In his first foray into writing for adults, Josh Clark proves he is more than up to the challenge, and delivers a spine-tingling debut thriller that demands to be experienced.

White
Feather
Press

It's the not-too-distant future, and in the wake of a nuclear terrorist attack, the President has signed the Freedom from Religion Act, which outlaws any public expression of religion. But what will the President do now that his wife and son are dead and he has converted to Christianity? Will he stand true to his newfound God, or will he buckle under political pressure? It was his lifelong dream to be President, but now he stands poised to lose it all, just for following the convictions of his heart.

White Feather Press

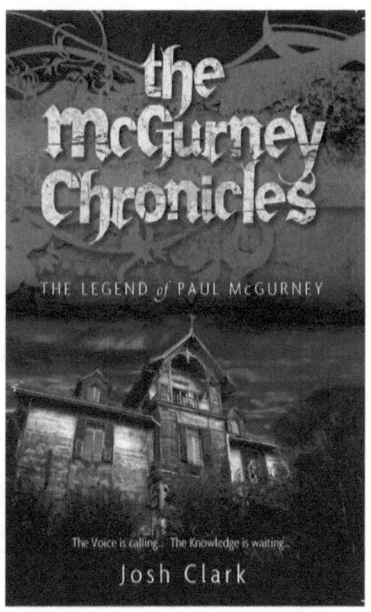

The Voice is Calling - The Knowledge is Waiting! When Todd, Zak, Jordan and Andrea agreed to spend the summer in their grandmother's remote cabin in the Colorado mountains, they had thought their biggest concern was death by boredom. Without video games, cell phone reception, or internet connection, the summer was supposed to be filled with leisurely naps by mountain streams and mundane hikes through wilderness trails. Boy were they wrong!

After stumbling upon a decrepit house on a forgotten hill, the children come face to face with Paul McGurney, a mysterious man with seemingly no past, who offers them a chance of a lifetime: a portal through time to bear witness to the life of the most famous man in history. But with this exclusive glimpse comes a hefty price, as an evil is unleashed who wants nothing more than to seek and destroy the children before they can fully experience what Paul McGurney is showing them.

White
Feather
Press